HIT & MISS

ALSO BY DEREK JETER

The Contract

Change Up

Derek Jeter's Ultimate Baseball Guide 2015

HIT & MISS

DEREK JETER

with Paul Mantell

JETER CHILDREN'S

SIMON & SCHUSTER BOOKS FOR YOUNG READERS

New York   London   Toronto   Sydney   New Delhi

SIMON & SCHUSTER BOOKS FOR YOUNG READERS
An imprint of Simon & Schuster Children's Publishing Division
1230 Avenue of the Americas, New York, New York 10020
This book is a work of fiction. Any references to historical events,
real people, or real places are used fictitiously. Other names, characters,
places, and events are products of the author's imagination, and any resemblance
to actual events or places or persons, living or dead, is entirely coincidental.
Text copyright © 2015 by Jeter Publishing, Inc.
Cover illustration copyright © 2015 by Mark Fredrickson
All rights reserved, including the right of reproduction
in whole or in part in any form.
SIMON & SCHUSTER BOOKS FOR YOUNG READERS
is a trademark of Simon & Schuster, Inc.
For information about special discounts for bulk purchases, please contact Simon
& Schuster Special Sales at 1-866-506-1949 or business@simonandschuster.com.
The Simon & Schuster Speakers Bureau can bring authors to your live event. For
more information or to book an event, contact the Simon & Schuster Speakers
Bureau at 1-866-248-3049 or visit our website at www.simonspeakers.com.
Also available in a Simon & Schuster Books for Young Readers hardcover edition
Book design by Krista Vossen
The text for this book was set in Centennial.
Manufactured in the United States of America
0716 OFF
First Simon & Schuster Books for Young Readers paperback edition August 2016
2 4 6 8 10 9 7 5 3 1
The Library of Congress has cataloged the hardcover edition as follows:
Jeter, Derek, 1974– author.
Hit & miss / Derek Jeter with Paul Mantell.
pages cm
Summary: Young Derek Jeter's friendship with a new student puts him
at odds with his friends and seems to be hurting his baseball swing, plus
he gets in trouble for confronting a student who is bullying his sister, in
violation of the contract with his parents.
ISBN 978-1-4814-2315-1 (hardback) — ISBN 978-1-4814-2316-8 (pbk)
ISBN 978-1-4814-2317-5 (eBook)
1. Jeter, Derek, 1974——Childhood and youth—Juvenile fiction. [1. Jeter, Derek,
1974——Childhood and youth—Fiction. 2. Baseball—Fiction. 3. Family life—Fiction.
4. Friendship—Fiction. 5. Bullying—Fiction.] I. Mantell, Paul, author. II. Title.
III. Title: Hit and miss.
PZ7.J55319Hit 2015
[Fic]—dc23
2015004818

To my family:

Thank you. For the conversations.

For being there when I looked up into the stands.

And for shaping my dream.

To my nephew, Jalen:

Dream away. It just might come true.

—D. J.

A Note About the Text

The rules of Little League followed in this book are the rules of the present day. There are six innings in each game. Every player on a Little League baseball team must play at least two innings of every game in the field and have at least one at bat. In any given contest, there is a limit on the number of pitches a pitcher can throw, in accordance with age. Pitchers who are eight years old are allowed a maximum of fifty pitches in a game, pitchers who are nine or ten years old are allowed seventy-five pitches per game, and pitchers who are eleven or twelve years old are allowed eighty-five pitches.

Dear Reader,

Hit & Miss is a book based on some of my experiences growing up and playing baseball. While I worked hard on the field, I was encouraged by my parents to do my best off the field as well, in my schoolwork and in supporting my team, teammates, and family.

I have tried to keep basic principles in mind as I work to achieve my dreams. This book is based on the second of those principles, which is to Think Before You Act. That is the theme of this book. I hope you enjoy it.

Derek Jeter

DEREK JETER'S 10 LIFE LESSONS

1. Set Your Goals High (*The Contract*)

2. **Think Before You Act** (*Hit & Miss*)

3. Deal with Growing Pains (*Change Up*)

4. Find the Right Role Models

5. The World Isn't Always Fair

6. Don't Be Afraid to Fail

7. Have a Strong Supporting Cast

8. Be Serious but Have Fun

9. Be a Leader, Follow the Leader

10. Life Is a Daily Challenge

CONTRACT FOR DEREK JETER

1. Family Comes First. Attend our nightly dinner.
2. Be a Role Model for Sharlee. (She looks to you to model good behavior.)
3. Do Your Schoolwork and Maintain Good Grades (As or Bs).
4. Bedtime. Lights out at nine p.m. on school nights.
5. Do Your Chores. Take out the garbage, clean your room on weekends, and help with the dishes.
6. Respect Others. Be a good friend, classmate, and teammate. Listen to your teachers, coaches, and other adults.
7. Respect Yourself. Take good care of your body and your mind. Avoid alcohol and drugs. Surround yourself with positive friends with strong values.
8. Work Hard. You owe it to yourself and those around you to give your all. Do your best in everything that you do.
9. Think Before You Act.

Failure to comply will result in the loss of playing sports and hanging out with friends. Extra-special rewards include attending a Major League Baseball game, choosing a location for dinner, and selecting another event of your choice.

CONTENTS

Chapter One—Season of Hope 1

Chapter Two—Welcome to the Red Sox 12

Chapter Three—The New Kid 21

Chapter Four—If at First You Don't Succeed . . . 30

Chapter Five—The House on the Hill 38

Chapter Six—Making Friends, Breaking Rules . . . 50

Chapter Seven—Play Ball! 62

Chapter Eight—Practice Makes Perfect? 78

Chapter Nine—The Swing Doctor 89

Chapter Ten—Game On! 98

Chapter Eleven—Patience Pays Off 109

Chapter Twelve—Push Comes to Shove 117

Chapter Thirteen—Breaking Through 127

Chapter Fourteen—Streak on the Line 134

Chapter Fifteen—On the Edge 141

Chapter Sixteen—Winner Takes All 149

Chapter Seventeen—Fore! 163

Chapter One

SEASON OF HOPE

"Derek!"

Derek threw down his pencil. He'd been doing his homework, even though it was only Saturday morning. Running to the top of the stairs, he looked down to see his father in the living room, holding a basketball.

"Almost finished, Dad. Just one more math problem." The rule in Derek's house was, you had to finish your homework *before* you were allowed to go play. It was right there in his contract with his parents, the one he'd signed the year before. He hadn't looked at it lately—his dad kept the original safe in his bedroom drawer—but Derek was pretty sure he remembered it all by heart.

"Perfect," his dad said. "I just finished one of my

homework assignments for this weekend too." He wasn't kidding. Charles Jeter was in his final year of classes at Western Michigan University, studying for a master's degree. His dream was to be a counselor for kids at risk, and Derek knew that meant a lot to his father, but being with his own kids was just as important to Derek's dad.

Derek could hardly wait. Basketball was fun, and he was proud of his progress over the winter. This was his chance to show his dad just how much better he'd gotten.

But the truth was, Derek's mind wasn't on basketball, and it wasn't on homework, either. Because today—this afternoon—was the start of the Little League baseball season. In fact, this afternoon was his first practice!

To Derek, no other sport was as important as baseball. His life's goal was to be the starting shortstop for the New York Yankees. He only hoped he still remembered how to hit, after the offseason.

For six months a year there wasn't much baseball being played in Kalamazoo, Michigan, where long snowy winters were the rule. His dad had taken him to the batting cages twice in the past two weeks, but it was still so cold out that every time Derek hit the ball, his hands stung.

"I thought you wanted to show me your new jump shot," his dad called after him with a little laugh. "You'd better get that math problem figured out."

Derek didn't take the time to answer. He went back to his desk, sat down, and concentrated, long enough to finish his homework and tie his sneakers. Then he raced downstairs to follow his dad, mom, and sister, Sharlee, out the door. They all piled into the family station wagon, and drove off to the university's outdoor basketball courts for a thrill-packed game of H-O-R-S-E!

Sharlee loved to be a part of their games, even if she was too little to put the ball into the basket without someone holding her up. Her usual job was ball-hawk, retrieving the balls that got away and bringing them back to the players.

Meanwhile, Mom did the scorekeeping, just to make sure there was no confusion or disagreement. She worked full-time as an accountant for a company, and she'd taught Derek to love math.

Derek was eager to show his family what he could do on the basketball court. He even dared to hope he would beat his dad at H-O-R-S-E, though he knew that wasn't likely. His dad was a really good athlete, and he was just as competitive as Derek.

Derek sometimes got frustrated when he lost, as he always seemed to. But he knew his dad would never lose on purpose just to make Derek happy. Derek didn't want to win that way anyhow. It wouldn't feel like winning, really. Every time he lost to his dad, it just made him want to work harder, so he could beat him the next time, or the time after that—or at least *someday*.

"Okay, you go first, Derek," his dad said. "Let's see what you've got."

Derek dribbled a couple of times, drove to the basket, did a 360-degree turn in midair, and sank the layup off the backboard. Then he turned to wink at Sharlee.

"Whoa!" his mom shouted. "Nice."

"Yay, Derek!" Sharlee yelled, giggling as she went to get the ball.

"Hey, now," Mr. Jeter laughed. "No playing favorites. Give me that ball, Sharlee. Here, old man. Let me show you how it's done."

He drove to the basket and easily made the same shot Derek had. Sharlee and Mrs. Jeter applauded, but not half as hard as for Derek.

"Okay. What else have you got?" he asked Derek.

This time Derek dribbled between his legs, pulled up, and sank a fifteen-foot jumper.

"All right, all right," Mr. Jeter said, nodding as Sharlee and Derek's mom whooped and hollered. He tried the between-the-legs move but got caught up and tangled, and the shot wasn't even close.

"That's *H* for you," Mrs. Jeter announced, pointing to her husband.

Derek made a move, froze, and sprung into the air, letting a shot fly. The ball swished right through the net. His dad's imitation came close but clanged off the rim and out.

"*H-O*," Mrs. Jeter called out. "Amazing, Derek!"

"Nice shot," said his dad. "I've got to hand it to you.

You're looking good there. Let's see if you can make that same one again."

Egged on by his dad, Derek took up the challenge. It was a long and difficult shot, but he'd learned to do it almost with his eyes closed. He lined it up, lifted off—but just as he was about to let it fly, Sharlee yelled, "Derek's gonna win!"

Her cry startled him, throwing his shot off by just enough for it to miss the rim. Derek groaned in frustration, but he didn't blame it on Sharlee. He knew she was only five and couldn't contain her excitement sometimes.

Now it was Mr. Jeter's turn. He did a double-fake quick drive to the basket, and then sank the layup from the far side with his left hand.

Derek gritted his teeth. He'd never made that shot yet. But he was determined to this time. Sharlee handed him the ball, and he made the double move—but lost control of the ball.

"Bzzzz!" his dad said, mimicking the buzzer.

"*H-O* to *H*," said Mrs. Jeter. "Getting interesting here."

Soon the game was tied, and then Derek fell behind by one letter. But Derek took advantage of a miss by his dad to throw in a hook shot from fifteen feet. Mr. Jeter couldn't match that one, and the game was tied again at *H-O-R*.

Suddenly Sharlee said, "Daddy, *I* want to shoot now."

"I know, Sharlee, but the game's not over yet," Mr. Jeter said. "When we're done, it'll be your turn."

"But I wanna shoot the ball!" Sharlee had a pretty good shot for a five-year-old, even if you did have to hold her up near the hoop. In fact, she was a really good overall athlete for her age.

It must be hard for her to watch other people play and not be part of it, Derek realized. Just then he saw his buddy Vijay riding by the courts on his bike. "It's okay, Dad," he said. "Let Sharlee shoot now. We'll take a time-out for a couple minutes."

Mr. Jeter saw Vijay, shrugged, and nodded. He bent down so that Sharlee could leap into his arms and take some shots. Mrs. Jeter got up and handed her the ball, while Derek turned and yelled, "Hey, Vij!" waving to get his friend's attention.

Vijay slowed his bike and came to a stop on the other side of the chain-link fence. His bike basket was filled with newspapers. Vijay had a morning route on Saturdays, delivering papers from Mount Royal Townhouses, where they both lived, all the way down the avenue to the university, about a mile away.

With the money he earned, he bought heaps of baseball cards. Vijay had the best collection in the neighborhood. He was baseball crazy, in fact, and it was all thanks to Derek, who'd taught him the game when Vijay and his family had first arrived in Kalamazoo.

"Hey, Derek," he called. "Where's your mitt? We've got practice this afternoon. Don't you want to warm up first?"

"Busy, Vij," Derek answered, nodding toward his family. "One last game of H-O-R-S-E. Gotta beat the big guy, show him who's got game."

"Oooh, I don't know, Derek," Vijay said, grinning but shaking his head. "Your dad is really good. No one can ever beat him."

"Not either of you guys, that's for sure," Mr. Jeter said, overhearing. "How 'bout it, old man? You quitting already?"

"Not a chance," Derek shot back.

"Guess who I found out is on our team," said Vijay. "Jeff Jacobson. And Jason and Isaiah, too. Practically our whole gang from the Hill!"

"Awesome," said Derek, excited. The year before, most of his friends had been on other teams. "Gotta go take care of business now, Vij. See you at the field."

"For sure. Go, Red Sox!"

"Ouch." Derek winced.

Why did his team have to be the Red Sox? As a passionate Yankees fan, he always rooted *against* the real Red Sox. And he'd *never* been on a team called the Yankees yet.

This would be the second year in a row that Derek and Vijay were on the same team. Vijay wasn't very good at sports, but Derek had worked with him on his baseball game, and he was definitely improving every year. And it was great that a bunch of their other friends were on the team.

"HEY!" Derek shouted as his dad stole the ball, taking advantage of Derek's mind wandering.

"Gotta pay attention!" Mr. Jeter said, sinking a perfect shot from the foul line. Derek figured it would be an easy shot to duplicate. But the "time-out" had somehow thrown him off his rhythm. To his and everyone else's surprise, he missed off the back rim.

"Point game," said his dad, cocking his head to one side.

"That's *H-O-R-S* for Derek," Mrs. Jeter announced. "*H-O-R* for you, Jeter."

"Jeter" was what she called her husband, and he called her "Dot," short for Dorothy. They both called Derek "old man," even though he wasn't a man yet—and he certainly wasn't old.

One more letter and his dad would win. *Again.* Derek gritted his teeth, determined not to go down without a fight.

They went at it for ten more minutes, both of them on fire, hitting shot after shot. Then, finally, Derek missed one. The ball went out of bounds, hitting the fence right next to Sharlee—but she didn't even budge to get it and throw it back to them.

"Come on, Sharlee. Let's have the ball," Mr. Jeter called to her.

But Sharlee wasn't listening. She was standing at the fence, staring across the street at two boys who were passing by. Derek noticed that one of the boys was looking back at her. He seemed older than Sharlee by a year or so, although he was almost Derek's size.

Sharlee had a frown on her face, and that was strange, because she was almost always happy and bubbly. "Hey, now," said Mr. Jeter. "What's the matter, Sharlee? Are you not feeling well?"

"I'm fine," Sharlee said. "FINE." She slowly turned back around. "I'm thirsty. Is there anything to drink?"

"I brought some juice," said Mrs. Jeter. "Here, come on and sit by me."

Sharlee went over to her mom and sat down. Derek turned to his dad. "What's up with her?" he asked.

"Beats me," said Mr. Jeter. "I've never seen her lose interest in a ball game like that."

"Me neither," Derek agreed. He looked down the street to where the two boys were walking. They were sharing a joke, it seemed, both of them laughing and looking back in Derek's direction.

"You don't have to talk about it if you don't want to," Mrs. Jeter told Sharlee. "But I hope you know that talking about things can help make them better."

"Come on, old man," Mr. Jeter said to Derek. "Let's finish this thing and see who's boss around here."

Derek knew his dad was saying they should give Sharlee some privacy with her mom. He also knew he had a chance to finally beat his dad at something!

That was before Mr. Jeter sank a thirty-footer, too long

a shot for Derek to hit. His shot fell two feet short, and the game was suddenly over.

Now it was Derek's turn to be sullen, but not for long. His dad came over to him and clapped him on the back. "Good game, old man. Your shot is getting there, it really is. Nice ballhandling, too. Very impressive."

It was a sincere compliment, and it made Derek feel much better about losing to his dad yet again.

In the car on the way home, Sharlee still seemed out of sorts. Derek wondered what had turned her from her usual self into this silent, sulking little girl. . . .

He was determined to find out, but for now he had to eat and get going. His new team was waiting for him, and he didn't want to be late!

His mom turned around in the front seat and said, "You know, Derek, I was looking at the Tigers' schedule for this season, and I saw that the Yankees are coming to town in the beginning of June."

It took him a second to realize she was talking about the major leagues, not Little League. "What? Mom, Dad, can we go? Can we, please?"

Derek loved nothing more than watching his beloved Yankees play, especially live. In the summers he often got to go to Yankee Stadium with his grandma, who lived in New Jersey and was the world's biggest Yankees fan.

But it was rare that the Yankees came to Detroit, usually only once a year.

"Well, let's see," said his mom. "Have you been keeping up with your contract?"

"Totally!" Derek said.

"Are you sure?" his dad asked. "When was the last time you read it over?"

"Um . . ."

"Not lately, I know that," Mr. Jeter said with a crooked grin. "Because I've got it in my drawer."

"I know it by heart!" Derek insisted. "And you know I've been doing good at following it."

"'Well,' not 'good,'" his mom corrected him.

"'Well,' I mean. So I think we should all sign a *new* contract, saying you agree to take me to the Yankees-Tigers game as a reward for keeping my *old* contract!"

His parents looked at each other and smiled. "Well, at least he's not afraid to stick up for himself," said Mrs. Jeter, and they all laughed—all except Sharlee.

"Okay, Derek, you've made your point," said his dad. "Never mind any new contracts. If you keep to all the rules between now and June, we'll take you to that game."

"Woo-hoo!" Derek yelled, exultant. He could feel the thrill of the coming baseball season coursing through him. The major-league season had started weeks ago, but today was the start of *his* baseball season.

He couldn't wait for practice to start!

Chapter Two

WELCOME TO THE RED SOX

Standing at shortstop on one of the four baseball diamonds that made up Westwood Fields, Derek looked around him and saw a team full of promise—even if the team did happen to be named the *Red Sox*.

Isaiah Martin was there with his full catcher's regalia—mask, shin protectors, chest protector, and big padded mitt. He, like Derek and Vijay, was one of the kids who played ball at Jeter's Hill—or, as Derek called it, simply "the Hill."

The grassy slope at Mount Royal Townhouses was the only place to play ball near their houses. The other kids had named it after Derek, who was there nearly every day except in the dead of winter.

Isaiah had been on the Tigers last year with Derek

and Vijay. He was a really good catcher. Not bad at hitting either, with some power and a good eye for balls and strikes.

Jeff, another regular from Jeter's Hill, was on the Red Sox too. He'd been on the champion Yankees last season, wearing Derek's favorite number—13—and playing Derek's favorite position, shortstop. Jeff had never really believed in Derek's dream of someday being shortstop for the New York Yankees. In fact, he'd regularly made fun of it.

But now they were going to be teammates, and that was a good thing, Derek thought—because no matter how much he shot his mouth off, Jeff could really pitch and hit, and he was a pretty good fielder, too.

Jason Rossini was another kid Derek knew from the Hill. He, too, had been a champion last year for the Yankees.

Man, thought Derek. *This team is loaded!*

He sort of knew Buster Murphy and Rocco Fanelli from Saint Augustine's. He was surprised to see that Rocco had enrolled in Little League, considering he usually showed zero interest in sports. "Murph," however, was pretty good at soccer and basketball, so maybe that meant he could play baseball, too.

Everyone else on the team was new to Derek, although he'd played against a few of them. He recognized a little speed demon who'd also been on the Yankees last year.

Sure, there were two or three kids who didn't seem to

be very good at fielding, but every team had some less talented players, even the best teams.

Last year Derek's Tigers hadn't been the strongest team. But they'd ended with a winning record. This year he was hoping for much more . . . maybe a championship, or at least a trip to the playoffs.

Beyond that, he wanted to make sure he got to play shortstop. Last year, because the coach's son had wanted the position, Derek had had to play second base for most of the season.

He concentrated hard now, knowing that first impressions mattered to coaches. Derek handled all his chances in the infield. He did well on fly balls to the outfield, too, although he had no desire to play there. He showed off his arm by uncorking a couple of rocket-like throws back to the infield, and he saw the coaches give each other wide-eyed looks.

During running drills he showed off his speed. Only the little skinny kid from last year's Yankees was faster. Again Derek saw that the coaches noticed.

This was going very well so far, he thought hopefully. Now if only he could impress them with his hitting. . . .

The head coach, Marty Kaufman, seemed like a nice man. He was tall and heavy, with a droopy mustache and long dark hair that stuck out from the back of his Red Sox cap.

His son, Miles, looked just like him except for the

mustache. Derek had already noticed that Miles wasn't a very good fielder. *Maybe he can hit,* thought Derek. In any case Derek was pretty sure Miles was not going to be competing with him for the shortstop job, and that was a big relief.

Derek waited patiently for his turn to hit. Coach Kaufman was doing the pitching for now, while his assistant coach, Mike Murphy, supervised the kids who were out in the field. Coach Murphy's son, Buster, was a tall kid too, even bigger than Miles.

Vijay stood two players ahead of Derek in line, waiting to hit. He was telling the two kids behind him all about Derek. "Did you know that he was the most valuable player in the all-star game last season? All-star! Most valuable!"

"Vijay, cut it out," Derek told him, embarrassed to be bragged about. He liked for his glove and his bat to do the talking for him.

"So modest," Vijay joked. "But come on, Derek, you know you're a great player."

"I'm okay," he answered, looking for a way to change the subject. "Hey, it's your turn, Vij. Let's see if you remember how to swing that bat."

He knew Vijay remembered. Twice in the past two weeks, Vijay had gone with Derek and his dad to the batting cages. Derek's parents were totally behind his baseball dreams, and they supported his friendships, too.

Vijay swung and missed at two easy pitches, before

finally connecting on one and sending a line drive to right field. "Attaboy," Derek said, clapping. "That's the stuff. Keep your eye on it."

Vijay hit a few more good balls, and then gave over to the next kid in line. As the next kid took his position in the batter's box, everyone turned to look, including Derek.

It wasn't that Derek knew every kid in the neighborhood, or that Kalamazoo was such a small town, but he'd seen every other kid in the league around town before, at least a few times. After all, he'd lived in Kalamazoo for the past five years.

This kid, he'd never seen in his entire life. He was built like an athlete, tall and thin, with a face full of freckles. He didn't seem to know how to stand at the plate. In fact, the kid seemed like he didn't know much about baseball at all.

During fielding practice, after making a nice catch of a sharp grounder at third, he'd hesitated, not knowing what to do next. Then he'd thrown the ball back to the catcher instead of to first base.

A few of the other kids had laughed and made comments, and the kid had looked painfully embarrassed.

As for hitting, his swing was powerful, but long and loopy. He swung through pitch after pitch, and Derek noticed some of the kids muttering to one another and shaking their heads.

Finally, on his last swing, the kid somehow connected

with a pitch that was way down in the dirt—and *wow*! The ball took off, high and far, and sailed for what seemed like miles.

"Whoa!" everyone said at once.

If he ever figures out how to make contact consistently, he's going to be really good, Derek thought. "Nice hit," he said.

The kid looked at him like he was from Mars. He didn't say anything. Not "thanks." Not a word.

"I'm Derek. Derek Jeter. What's your name?"

The kid looked away. "Dave."

"Nice to meet you, Dave."

The kid made no reply. He just walked over to the bench, sat down, and stared at the dirt between his feet.

Strange, thought Derek. *Well, maybe he's shy or something.*

Derek turned his attention to the next hitter, Reggie Brown. Reggie had been in Derek's class last year. He had asthma and carried an inhaler around with him that he used once in a while to help him breathe. Derek hoped Reggie didn't have to use it during a game, while running the bases or something. *It must be tough to have a hard time breathing,* he thought.

Reggie hit a few pop-ups, a grounder, and one good line drive. Then it was Derek's turn.

He stepped to the plate and suddenly felt energized. It was as if the entire winter had shrunk down to the size of a pea, and the all-star game that had ended last season had taken place only yesterday.

He whacked the first pitch so hard that Coach Kaufman had to hit the dirt. "Wow! Easy there!" he joked as he got up and dusted himself off.

Derek then proceeded to hit the next three pitches over the outfielders' heads. He finished off with two sharp grounders and another screamer past the mound.

He handed the bat to the next kid and dusted off his hands. He could feel his heart pounding with excitement, and something else—*relief.*

Those two sessions in the batting cages had really gotten him ready, and he'd made exactly the first impression he'd wanted to make.

"What did I tell you?" Vijay was crowing to the kids around him. "Derek's the best. We can't lose!"

"Hey," Derek corrected him. "Don't jinx us. The season hasn't even started yet." But he had to admit, the Red Sox looked pretty good, better than any team he'd been on up till now, that was for sure!

After practice all the kids scattered. Those who lived near Westwood Fields walked, and the rest got into their parents' cars and drove away. Derek saw his mom waiting for him in the old station wagon.

"Come on, Vijay. Let's go," Derek said. Mrs. Jeter usually drove Vijay home, since his family lived in Mount Royal

Townhouses, and the two families knew each other well.

As they walked toward the car, Derek saw the new kid, Dave, standing alone, far from the other stragglers who were hanging out together, talking and joking around. He was staring at the ground, looking lost and sad. It reminded Derek of how Sharlee had looked that morning.

"Strange, huh?" Vijay said.

"What?"

"That new kid."

"You mean Dave?" Derek asked.

"That's his name? Dave?"

"That's what he said."

"Dave what?"

"He didn't say," Derek said. "In fact, Dave was the only word he said."

"Nobody on the team has ever seen him before," Vijay said. "I asked everyone."

"Maybe he's new in town," Derek suggested.

"Or maybe he lives somewhere else and his parents gave a false address so he could play in our league. It happens, you know."

Derek gave Vijay a look. "Yeah, right. And maybe I'm a space alien. Come on, Vij. Get real."

"Well, he doesn't seem very happy to be here, that's for sure," said Vijay, opening the car door.

"Oh well," said Derek, sitting down across from Vijay in the backseat. "I guess we'll find out his story sooner or later."

"Hi, guys. How was practice?" asked Mrs. Jeter.

"Fine," said Derek.

"Great!" said Vijay. "This is going to be a great team."

"Wow!" said Derek's mom. "Sounds promising."

"We'll see," Derek cautioned. "So far so good, but—"

"But what?" Vijay asked.

"You never know," Derek answered, then gave his friend a little smile. "Hey, that's why we play the games, right?"

Chapter Three

THE NEW KID

"Okay, class. Attention, please."

At the sound of Mr. Beckham's voice, Derek looked up from the composition he was writing. It was about the Revolutionary War, from the point of view of a colonist loyal to the king of England.

Mr. Beckham had left the room for a few minutes while they'd been working, and he now came back in with Dave, the new kid from Derek's team.

Dave stood next to Mr. Beckham and a step behind him, looking uncomfortable. His eyes darted this way and that, and he kept his hands folded in front of him, rocking forward and backward on his feet.

"This is David Hennum, class."

"Um, it's . . . Dave," murmured Dave, staring at the floor.

"Ah. Okay. Dave, then. He and his family have just moved here, from Beverly Hills, California, of all places."

Mr. Beckham smiled, his eyebrows raised. But if this juicy nugget had been intended to impress the class, it had the opposite effect. Giggles and murmurs filled the room. Derek heard the words "Mr. Hollywood" and "snob," among others.

"Calm down, class," Mr. Beckham said, clapping his hands twice to restore order. When the noise quieted down, he went on to say, "I know you'll show him a warm Saint Augustine's welcome. Right?"

"Right!" Derek said. Then he realized that he was one of only two or three kids to answer, with the others keeping an embarrassed silence. Derek slunk down in his chair as more giggling and murmuring started.

Mr. Beckham frowned. "Let me ask again. *Right?*"

This time the class responded as requested. But Derek knew, and was sure Dave knew too, that they didn't really mean it.

He could see that Dave had become even more uncomfortable. Mr. Beckham directed him to an empty seat in the back row, where Dave was not heard from at all the rest of that morning.

From time to time one or another of the kids would lean over and whisper something to his or her neighbor, like,

"Where are his cool shades?" or "He doesn't *look* famous," or "I'll bet he's a snob."

Derek didn't respond. He focused on his work, but every now and then he would glance behind him at Dave. It seemed as if everyone else was doing the same thing. Dave, for his part, kept his eyes firmly planted on his desk. Finally, mercifully, the bell rang for recess.

It was warm and sunny outside. The last of the snow piles in the corner of the schoolyard had shrunken to almost nothing. Derek sat on a bench, eating the sandwich and apple that his mom had packed for him.

As the kids who ate in the cafeteria filtered out into the schoolyard for the second half of recess, several groups started playing games—everything from freeze tag, to marbles, to throwing around a football, to soccer. Other kids just hung out together around the edges of the schoolyard, talking in groups or pairs.

Vijay and Isaiah called Derek over to where they were discussing the team's chances. "That kid Cubby can really play," Isaiah was saying. "He stole home twice last year, I heard."

"I know he made the all-star team," Derek said.

"He break-dances, too," Vijay said. "He's in public school, but they have a talent show, just like here at Saint Augustine's."

"Break-dances, huh?" Derek said with a laugh. "That's cool."

"Have you ever tried it?" Vijay asked. "I bet you could bust some moves."

"Cut it out," Derek said, giving Vijay a playful elbow. "I'd like to see you try that stuff."

"Him?" That made Isaiah crack up. Vijay didn't seem like the type to break-dance, but Derek knew that people sometimes surprised you, so it was better not to assume anything.

"Hey, I can do whatever I set my mind to. Right, Derek?" Vijay said.

"Right." Derek wasn't going to say no. Vijay had always supported Derek's dream. Derek owed him at least the same in return.

"It's just not my thing," Vijay concluded.

"There you go," said Isaiah.

Derek glanced over Isaiah's shoulder and saw that Dave was sitting alone again. He had his elbows resting on his knees, and his chin resting in his hands.

Derek's memories of his own first days in Kalamazoo came flooding back to him. Most people had welcomed the Jeters, an interracial family, with smiles and open arms when they'd arrived from the East Coast. But a few people hadn't.

It hadn't been easy for Derek in the beginning—or for Vijay, either. The Patels had been the first Indian American family to move into Mount Royal Townhouses. Derek and Vijay had made friends right away, but it had taken a while for Vijay's parents to fit in.

"Hey, guys, you want to go over and talk to the new kid?" Derek asked his friends.

"Sure, why not?" said Vijay, who was always game for anything Derek suggested.

"I don't know," Isaiah said.

"He's on our team *and* in our class," Derek reminded him.

"Yeah, but he doesn't seem very friendly," Isaiah said.

"Sometimes you've got to make the first move," Derek said with a little grin. "Like in break dancing. Right, Vijay?"

They all laughed. Then the bell rang for the end of recess.

Taking the first step with Dave would have to wait until after school. Isaiah and Vijay both looked relieved, but Derek was determined to break the ice. It was what *he* would have wanted someone to do for him on *his* first day in a new school.

"I got a ninety-three."

It was the end of the school day, and Derek was standing near the main entrance of the school, comparing test results with Gary Parnell, the smartest kid in fourth grade. Gary had been in his class last year too, and the two boys had been rivals for almost two years running.

Gary made a big show of pulling his test paper out of his book bag. "Read it and weep, Jeter," he said with a satisfied grin.

"Ninety-eight. Nice work, Gary." Derek handed the paper back to him. "Watch out next time, though. I'm getting closer."

"In your dreams," said Gary, tucking the precious paper back into his bag, which was full of such papers.

Gary never got tired of rubbing it in. Derek had beaten him on a test only once, but that had been such a sweet victory that Derek had been working twice as hard ever since to beat him again, just to see that shocked look on Gary's face one more time.

Derek saw Dave duck out the main door. "I've got to go, Gary. See you tomorrow."

"Yeah. Science test! Can't wait." He rubbed his hands together, imagining another victory over Derek.

"Me neither."

Derek smiled right back at him, mustering enough confidence that Gary was taken aback, at least for a moment. Then Gary laughed and nodded. "Okay, game on then, Jeter. See you tomorrow." He gave Derek a little fist pound and headed down the street.

"Hey, Dave, wait up!" Derek called, turning.

Dave, who had been walking toward the far end of the parking lot at a brisk pace, stopped and frowned when he saw Derek jogging toward him. He jutted his chin out and said, "What do you want?"

"Whoa." Derek was thrown off balance. "I just wanted to see how you were doing."

Dave screwed his face up into a skeptical look. "What, did Mr. Beckham tell you to go make friends with the new kid?"

"Huh? No! No way. He didn't say anything. I just—I . . ."

Derek fell silent as words failed him. What had he been trying to do, anyway? Suddenly he felt foolish and wished he'd just left Dave to himself.

"Okay, thanks for asking. I'm fine. See you." Dave turned to go.

"Wait! Um, I just wanted to say, nice hit the other day at practice."

Dave snorted. "Yeah. The one ball I made contact with. I whiffed on, what, seven?"

"And you snagged that ball at third. That was awesome."

"Right before I threw it to the wrong guy," Dave added. "Listen, seriously, thanks for trying, but you know as well as I do that I barely know the rules of the game."

"Oh. Well, that's not hard. I could teach you. I—"

"Thanks, but I've gotta go. My ride is here."

"Oh. I thought you were walking," Derek said.

"Nah. I live too far away."

"Oh yeah? Where?"

Dave opened his mouth to reply, but then stopped himself. "I've gotta go. Bye."

He turned and ran to the edge of the parking lot, then passed through the gate that led out onto the street. An incredibly fancy car waited there, complete with a driver in a black suit and a cap with a shiny visor!

Dave opened the rear door and got in. As the driver pulled away, Derek just stood and stared.

"Whaaat?" It was Vijay, who had come up behind Derek unseen. "Did you see that?"

"Unreal, huh?"

"I think that was a Mercedes."

"Huh?"

"Mercedes. Haven't you heard of them? They're, like, super expensive. That kid must be *soooo rich*."

"Looks that way."

The two boys headed back toward the main entrance, where the bus was waiting to take them back to Mount Royal Townhouses. On the bus everybody was talking about the new kid.

"It was a Mercedes, man," Jeff was saying to Isaiah. "The biggest model Mercedes."

"Naw, I think it was a Rolls-Royce or something. And did you see the *driver*?"

"Hey, how do you know that wasn't his dad?" Derek butted in.

"Dads don't wear caps with visors when they drive," said Jeff.

One kid put on a pair of sunglasses, stuck out his hand, and mimicked being Dave, saying, "You can all kiss my Oscar now." This brought on gales of laughter from the kids sitting nearby.

Derek took a seat next to the mimic, while Vijay found a

seat two rows back. Derek sat there, hearing the mockery and jokes about Dave but tuning them out.

He felt bad for Dave, that was the truth. He'd been made fun of himself back in the day, and as young as he had been at the time, the memory was still fresh in his mind.

Maybe the kids were right. Maybe Dave was an impossible, stuck-up snob. But one way or the other, Derek was determined to try reaching out to him again. There had to be a way to break through Dave's hostile armor and let him know someone understood.

He just hoped Dave's feelings weren't already crushed beyond repair.

Chapter Four

IF AT FIRST YOU DON'T SUCCEED . . .

"Hey, are you trying to take my head off?"

Derek grinned as he rounded first base and Jason barked at him playfully. Derek's liner had come awfully close to beaning Jason, who had ducked out of the way just in time, letting the ball go past him into right field.

Derek stopped at second, seeing the throw come in from right. "You're supposed to catch it in your mitt, not in your teeth," Derek explained, putting his two hands together as if to catch a ball.

"I'm not catching anything going that fast," Jason shot back, laughing. "Why don't you hit it like that during the season, instead of trying to kill your teammates in practice?"

"Ha!" Derek shook his head and laughed.

Jason was funny, and Derek knew how to shoot the jokes as well as anyone else. He and his dad had been ribbing each other that way ever since Derek was old enough to hold a ball in his hands. It was part of competing, the part where you could let loose a little of the tension between games or between innings.

The Red Sox were having a scrimmage today, with the team divided into two squads, and a few players from each side switching back and forth so there were always enough players on the field.

Derek liked the way Coach Kaufman ran things. Unlike last year's coach, he didn't seem to be holding auditions for the various positions. He was just letting the kids catch, throw, run, and hit—and he was paying close attention.

Not just that. By holding this scrimmage, the coach was already assigning kids to positions, and places in the batting order, to see how they fit there.

What Derek liked best about it was that he himself had been assigned to play shortstop, and to hit third in the lineup. That suited him fine. In fact, it was just about perfect!

The next hitter up was Dave. He had already made a mental mistake at third base, forgetting to tag a runner when there was no force play on.

It was obvious to one and all that Dave hadn't played organized baseball before—*ever*. Derek guessed he would figure out the rules of baseball sooner or later. But Derek knew it could be sooner if Dave would only let him help!

Dave whiffed on the first pitch to him, then whiffed again. Both pitches had been right over the plate. "He can't hit a lick," Jason said.

"He looks good swinging, though," Jeff said. He was playing second. "He just doesn't make any contact."

"Not even close," Jason agreed.

Derek felt bad. If he could hear them from his lead off second, Dave could probably hear them from home plate.

"He hit it great that one time," Derek reminded them as Dave whiffed on a third straight pitch to end the inning.

"I know, it's true," Jason agreed as he headed back to the dugout. "But will he ever hit another one?"

The scrimmage went on for another half hour. Derek got to bat twice more and wound up with two doubles and a triple, all on screaming line drives the other way. His work in the batting cages had really paid off, and Derek was psyched about the team's upcoming first game.

He was even more psyched when Coach Kaufman agreed to let him wear number 13—Derek's dad's number when he was in college! He had wanted to wear 13 last year but had been stuck with number 2, much to his disappointment. Everything this season seemed to be going his way, at least so far.

Derek couldn't help noticing, though, that Dave wasn't having such an easy time of it. He made no contact that whole day—either with the baseball or with the other kids on the team.

On the bench he sat alone and silent while everyone else joked around, cheered, or talked baseball. After practice he stood alone, just like the first time. Derek figured he was waiting for the Mercedes, or whatever it was, to pick him up. Sure enough, Derek saw it parked just around the corner on a side street, obviously in an attempt to avoid attention.

Too bad for Dave that they'd already seen it. Now everybody knew he was rich, and they assumed he didn't want to talk to any of them.

Derek wasn't one of those kids, though. And he wanted to make sure Dave knew it. Derek raced over to where his dad was waiting, having just arrived in the family station wagon.

"How'd it go?" asked Mr. Jeter.

"Excellent." Derek held up the number 13 jersey and grinned. "And I got to play short, and I went three for three, but I've got to go talk to somebody. Can you wait five more minutes, Dad? It's important." Dave was already quite a distance away, walking slowly down the street toward the corner where the car sat idling.

"All right," his dad said, sounding unsure. "But make it quick. I've got a school assignment to finish."

Derek really appreciated that his parents both took the time to make sure he and Sharlee got to all their activities. He knew they were busy and could easily have made excuses for not being available. But they never did. In fact, they stayed throughout the game, practice, or other event whenever they could—which was most of the time. Derek always felt like whatever happened, he and his family were always all in it together.

"Hey, Dave—wait up!"

Dave turned and saw Derek running toward him at full speed. He heaved a big sigh and put his hands on his hips.

"What do you want now?" he asked as Derek caught up to him just before he turned the corner.

"Gee," Derek said. "I was just trying to see if you wanted to be friends or something. You act like you've got a problem with that."

Dave snorted. "Yeah, right. Like I believe that."

"How about you tell me why you don't believe it," Derek said.

"You're just trying to find out stuff about me so you can tell everyone. Then you can all make fun of me some more."

"You think you're the only one who ever got messed with?" Derek said angrily. "My mom's white, and my dad's black. We came here when I was four, and we got some dirty looks. A few people called us names. . . . It really hurt."

Dave swallowed hard. "Wow. That totally bites. I'm so sorry, man."

Derek grinned. "I asked my mom and dad about it, and

they told me to hold my head up and be proud of who I was. I didn't let anyone's comments get to me. And pretty soon I got to find out how awesome most people around here really are."

"Wow," Dave said, shaking his head. "I'm really sorry I got you wrong, Dirk."

"Derek."

"Sorry, Derek. I just— It's been so . . ."

"I didn't keep my dad waiting in the car just to come up here and make fun of you, if that's what you're thinking."

"No, no." Dave looked at Derek as if he'd never seen him before "Thanks for being straight up about stuff," he said. "You're the first one who didn't treat me like I'm some kind of weirdo. Everyone's been laughing at me behind my back."

"Aw, they're just goofing around. They'll be fine once they get to know you."

"If that ever happens." Dave heaved another sigh. "I know what they all think of me."

"Oh yeah? What's that?" Derek asked.

"That I'm this rich snob from Hollywood who thinks he's somebody special," Dave said.

"Well, you are from Hollywood, right?"

"Beverly Hills, actually."

"Same difference," Derek said. "And as far as being rich . . ."

"You mean the Mercedes? It's my mom's. She works for

this big corporation and gets driven everywhere."

"Nice."

"Yeah, except that's why we had to move here. Relocation to the Midwest district or something."

"Kalamazoo's a great place," Derek said encouragingly. "You'll see. Pretty soon it'll feel like home to you."

"Not like California. It's warm there all year round—" The horn sounded, interrupting them. "I've gotta go," Dave said.

"Right."

"Well, thanks for reaching out, Derek. At least now I know there's someone who doesn't hate me."

"Just the first of many soon to come," Derek said, turning to go. "You'll see."

"Hey, listen—you . . . you mentioned you might be able to help me get better at this game. . . . You really think you could?"

"I . . . I could try," Derek said. He was pretty sure he could, but he didn't want Dave to blame him if it didn't work out well.

"I mean, you seem like you know what you're doing. Me, I haven't got a clue, in case you haven't noticed."

"I figured you hadn't played much before," Derek said, shrugging.

"Like, never," Dave said with a laugh. "So, you want to?"

"Sure," Derek said, feeling triumphant. He'd done it! He'd broken through Dave's armor and made a friend.

"You can come over to the Hill after school tomorrow. Me and my friends are there pretty much every day."

Dave's smile faded. "Oh," he said. "Um, I was sort of hoping you could come over to my house."

"Well, my folks will want to talk to your folks first. Why don't you come over to the Hill tomorrow, and next time I'll come to your house."

"Okay. Where is it?"

"Mount Royal Townhouses. It's the only hill in sight, even though it's not much of one. You'll see us there. Just bring your mitt."

"Okay, deal," said Dave.

"See you tomorrow," Derek said. Knowing his dad was waiting for him, he turned and ran back to the station wagon.

As he settled into his seat, his dad asked, "So? How'd it go?"

"Really, really good," Derek said.

Between having a great practice and making a brand-new friend, today had been a *very* good day.

Chapter Five

THE HOUSE ON THE HILL

"Dude, why'd you invite *him*?" Jeff rolled his eyes and waited for Derek's reply.

"Come on," Derek said. "What do you guys have against Dave?"

"Do we need a reason? Okay, how about, he thinks he's all that?" Jeff said. Behind him, Jason and Isaiah nodded their agreement as they ate their sandwiches in the schoolyard.

Derek looked over at Vijay to see if he agreed with the others, but Vijay just looked at the ground. He seemed to be wrestling with something inside himself.

"You guys don't even know him," Derek said. "You're just assuming stuff about him because he's new—"

"And because he's from Hollywood—" Jeff said.

"Beverly Hills," Derek corrected him.

"Same difference," Jason insisted. "Plus, he rides around in a Mercedes, with a driver, *and*—"

"Like I say, you don't know anything about him," Derek repeated. "That's why I figured I'd invite him over to the Hill."

Derek was the one originally responsible for turning the Hill into their baseball field. It wasn't exactly suitable—a slope of grass with two big trees in left and right field, and bumps everywhere. But it was the best spot available, so it had to do.

You could always count on finding Derek there, looking for a pickup game of baseball—or at least a simulated game, complete with Derek announcing the play by-play.

"The kid doesn't have cooties, you know. He's just new and doesn't have any friends yet."

"So you have to be the first?" Jeff asked.

"Hey, you know what? You shouldn't judge people before you know them," Derek shot back. "He might be really cool."

"Yeah, right. Too cool for anybody here," Isaiah said.

"He probably won't even come," Jason said.

"He seemed like he was going to," Derek replied. "Anyhow, if he comes, we can help him improve his game."

"We'd *better* help him, if we expect the team to be any good," said Isaiah. He meant the Red Sox.

"Where is he, anyway?" Vijay asked.

"Over there, in the far corner," Derek said, gesturing with his head to where Dave sat eating alone.

"Did you see what he eats for lunch?" Isaiah asked. "It's like a gourmet meal and stuff."

"He probably has a food taster," Jason joked, and all the boys laughed—except for Derek, who just shook his head.

He could still remember being on the other end of those kinds of jokes—even though it had been a couple years since he'd been the new kid at Saint Augustine's.

What puzzled him was Vijay. He laughed along with the rest of the boys, although he'd been the new kid once too. Derek was sure he still remembered. So what was going on with *him*?

The bell rang, and everyone started filing back toward the doors. "Well, I guess it's okay if he shows up," Jeff said. "I just hope it doesn't wind up being a snobfest."

When the bell rang to end the school day, Dave came over to Derek's desk with a big smile on his face.

"Hey, Derek," he said. "You ready?"

"Huh? Ready for what?"

"Come with me. I've got a surprise for you." Dave led him down the school's front steps and across the lawn, toward the hedge where the Mercedes had been waiting the other day.

"Hey, listen," Derek said. "I've gotta catch the bus . . ."

"Just a second," Dave insisted, not slowing down. Derek had no choice but to follow him.

They wound up in front of the Mercedes, just as Derek had expected. The driver, dressed in a dark suit and wearing his visored cap, was holding the rear door open.

"Hello there, young man," he greeted Derek. "My name is Chase." He gave a little nod of the head and offered his hand. "Chase Bradway."

"Derek," Derek answered, shaking the driver's hand. "Derek Jeter. Pleased to meet you, Mr. Bradway."

"Just call me Chase. Everyone else does." He gave Derek a tip of his cap and a smile.

"Go on," Dave said. "Get in."

"Huh? Oh!" Derek was completely taken by surprise. "Um, I don't know . . ."

Actually, he *did* know—or at any rate, he was pretty sure—that his parents would not approve of him getting into someone else's car without their knowing about it.

"It's okay. Chase is a really careful driver. He'll get us there safely."

Oh well, he thought. *What harm could it do?* Mount Royal Townhouses were only about half a mile away. He and Dave would just get to the Hill that much faster. They'd be waiting there when the bus dropped the other kids off.

Derek shrugged. "I've never ridden in a car like this before. It's practically a limo."

"Ah, yeah." Dave nodded with a smile—the first smile Derek had ever seen on his face. It looked like it belonged there, but it lasted only a second. "I remember when I thought it was a big deal. You can get used to anything, believe me."

"I wouldn't mind getting used to it," Derek said with a laugh, throwing caution to the wind as he got in and sat down on the plush leather seat. "I'd want to drive it myself, though."

"Totally," said Dave, sitting next to Derek. The driver shut the door and got in the front seat. Again Derek felt a pang of . . . of something. Was it remorse? Dread? His guilty conscience?

They rolled slowly past the front of the school building. Everyone stared at the car, with Derek in it, his face pressed to the window. He grinned and waved, but most of the kids just shook their heads in surprise.

"It's a 500 SEL," Dave told him, patting the seat. "Soon as I'm old enough, I'm telling Chase to move over and let me drive this baby. Right, Chase?"

"Soon as you have a license," said Chase. "And oh, by the way, Dave, I seem to recall that you have two more tests coming up this week—social studies and English—and I'm expecting you to leave plenty of time for studying today, as well as homework."

"Okay, Chase," Dave said, rolling his eyes and shooting

Derek a smile. "I'll get it done. No worries."

"See that you do. And how are your grades, young man?" he asked Derek.

"Me? Oh, um, they're pretty good, I guess. Nineties most of the time."

"Good man," said Chase. "Keep it up."

Derek was surprised that Chase had asked. But he knew his parents would have wanted to know the same thing about Dave. Except, Chase was Dave's *driver*, not his dad. . . . What was going on?

Suddenly Derek noticed that the street outside the car window was unfamiliar. "Hey!" he said. "I think we passed Mount Royal Townhouses."

Dave smiled. "That's the other half of the surprise," he told Derek. "We're going to my house!"

"What?"

"I know, but don't worry—you can call your parents when we get there and tell them where we are. And Chase will drive you right home to your door afterward."

"But—"

"Quit worrying, okay? You can blame it on me. Tell them your new friend kidnapped you." He laughed, and Derek couldn't help joining in.

Derek bit his lip. He didn't want to make things awkward for Dave. He knew it must have taken a big leap for Dave to put himself out there like this.

Derek didn't want to make it seem like he was inventing an excuse not to hang out with Dave either. It did seem like a harmless adventure, after all. And Dave had actually called Derek his friend!

Derek told himself he would just call his mom and dad when he got to Dave's house, and let them speak to Dave's parents.

He sat back and looked out the window as they wound down a curving road and through a patch of woods, and then emerged on the shore of a beautiful lake. There, across the lake, was a large house—you could even call it a mansion—with a sloping lawn leading down to the lakeshore.

"That's your house?" Derek said, openmouthed.

"Well, it's the corporation's, technically," Dave said. "But we get to live there—at least until my mom gets transferred to some other place."

"Which is how long?" Derek wondered.

Dave shrugged. "Who knows? We were in LA for five years. Before that, Hawaii for three. Before that, well . . . I was just a baby back then."

Chase pulled the car to a stop in front of the house, then got out. He opened the car door for the boys, and they piled out. Derek realized his mouth was wide open as he stared at the gigantic stone house. It looked like a kind of castle from the Middle Ages or something.

"Come on in, and I'll show you around," said Dave, waving

for Derek to follow him up the front steps to the huge oaken door under the stone archway. "It really is impressive."

"Thanks, Mr. Bradway," Derek said to the driver.

"You can call me Chase," he corrected Derek. "And no need for thanks, young man. I'm just doing my job." He gave Derek a smile and a nod, clapped Dave affectionately on the back, and said, "Don't forget about your homework. And those tests."

"No, sir," said Dave with a smile and a little salute. "Come on, Derek. Let me show you the house."

Chase turned away and busied himself polishing the car's hood.

"What's with the salute?" Derek asked as they went up the marble steps to the front door.

"Oh. Chase is ex–Green Beret," Dave explained. "Special Forces. He has these medals from the Vietnam War—you should see them."

"Wow. That's pretty incredible. Is he, like, related to you or something?"

Dave laughed. "Sort of. Not really, but he might as well be. I see more of him than I do either of my folks."

"Sure seems like it," said Derek.

"He's officially my mom's driver. But he's really much more than that. He actually started out as the head of my dad's security detail."

"Security detail?"

"Yeah. My dad's with something called the World Bank. He travels a lot, to different countries, so they gave him a security detail. But I guess he was worried about me and my mom being safe while he was overseas. So he asked Chase to stay with Mom and me. And he's been part of the family ever since."

Derek realized that Dave's dad must have been really important to need his own security detail.

"Everyone had drivers in Beverly Hills, so I never really thought about it being weird or anything, until we moved to Kalamazoo."

"Huh. Well, it's definitely not like that here," said Derek. "I don't think there's one other person in this whole town who's got a driver, and not too many with a great big Mercedes, either."

Dave opened the door and led Derek inside, where a grand marble hallway with ceilings three stories high greeted them.

"Wow," Derek said.

"Yeah, I know," Dave agreed. "It's amazing. Too bad it's not really ours. Technically the corporation owns it."

Derek didn't reply. He was too busy gawking as Dave led him through the living rooms, kitchen, sunroom, and several other spaces, each more extravagant than the last.

"Everyone always tells me not to touch anything," Dave said with a grin, touching an antique desk just to show he could, and winking at Derek. "So I guess you'd better keep your paws off everything too."

Derek laughed but made a mental note to be careful around all these expensive things. "Hey, listen, I'd better call home. My folks will want to check in with your parents."

Dave blinked. "My parents? Oh, they're not here."

"What?" Derek felt a knot develop suddenly in the pit of his stomach. He had just assumed that at least one of Dave's parents would be here to supervise them.

"Like I told you, Chase is sort of part of the family," Dave explained. "He's always in charge of me whenever my parents are away."

"Away?"

"Yeah, my mom's in London and my dad's in Singapore or someplace."

"Wow . . . um, what does your mom do?" Derek asked.

"She works for an international computer company. 'Executive vice president of media relations,' whatever that means," Dave replied. "Now she's got the whole Midwest as her territory, so she's on the road half the time. My dad's away even more than that. I've got no brothers or sisters. So like I said, Chase and I are stuck with each other a lot of the time."

"Wow."

What else could Derek say? On the one hand Dave's

family sure sounded every bit as rich as all the kids imagined they were. On the other hand Derek felt a little sorry for him. It sounded like he didn't get to spend much time with his parents. Derek couldn't imagine living like that. He and his family were as close as—well, as *family*!

"Was it like that in California, too?" Derek asked.

"Nah, that's where my grandparents live, so they were over at the house whenever my folks went somewhere."

"Ah."

Derek wondered what he should do now. Probably ask to be driven home right away. But he didn't want to do that. That would make Dave think Derek was weird, or that Derek didn't like him or something. Which wasn't true at all. Derek was actually starting to think Dave was a pretty cool kid.

Maybe he should call home now and let his parents talk to Chase. But Derek quickly backed off that idea. They wouldn't understand about a driver being a substitute parent. Not unless he explained it to them first—and in person, not over the phone.

In the end Derek decided to tell them all about it when he got home, and let them talk to Chase afterward. It wasn't a good solution, but at this point he couldn't think of a better one.

"Come on, I'll show you my rooms," Dave said.

"Rooms? There's more than one?" Derek couldn't

believe what he was seeing. If the other kids could see all this, they would think Dave was from another planet.

Dave might have been living the lifestyle of the rich and famous, but Derek could tell that he was down to earth. He was treating Derek like a *friend*. Like an *equal*.

Chapter Six

MAKING FRIENDS, BREAKING RULES

"It's a mess," Dave said. "Staff or no staff, my parents want me to clean my own room."

"Mine too. My sister, Sharlee, and I have lots of chores around the house."

"Yeah, but I have *two* rooms to clean. Come on in here."

He led Derek through the actual bedroom—with its double bed, desk, mini electric car set, clothes all over the floor—into another large room, covered in green outdoor carpeting, with little humps built into it and a hole sunk into the middle.

"What's this?" Derek asked. "It looks like a miniature golf hole."

"It *is*!" Dave said excitedly. "It's a putting green."

"That's way cool," Derek said, shaking his head in wonder. "I can't believe this. Was this here when you moved in?"

"No, my parents put it in for me."

"Wow."

"See . . . I'm really into golf." Dave looked at Derek like he was sharing a big secret with him.

"*Golf?* Wow. I've never met anybody who was into golf before. I thought it was just for rich—" He quickly stopped himself. "Oh. Right."

"Everybody in Beverly Hills plays. Even the kids. And my dad's into it big time. Half his business trips are golf outings. He took me golfing from the age of four. I got my first set of clubs at six."

"No way," Derek said, astonished. "Aren't those—" He stopped himself before saying "expensive."

"You want to try some putts?" Dave asked him.

"Sure." Derek took a few putts, and sank one, but the rest were either too weak or too strong, or off to the side of the cup. "I'll bet you're way better at this stuff," he said, handing the putter back to Dave.

Dave took it and proceeded to sink six straight putts. "I'm getting there," he said with a grin—a real one this time, one that lasted at least five seconds.

"You should see the setup we've got out back," he told Derek, laying the putter down and leading his guest back downstairs.

They went out the back door. To call it a backyard would not have been fair. What Derek was gazing at was more like a park. There was a tennis court, a swimming pool, and another putting green—this one made out of real grass.

There was also a big cage with netting on three sides. "What's that for?" Derek asked. "T-ball?" It reminded him of the nets at the batting cages where he went with his dad.

"No, man. It's for driving," Dave said.

"Driving?"

"Not cars—golf balls."

"Ooohh." Derek thought for a moment. "I wonder why it's called 'driving' instead of just 'hitting.'"

"Well, when you tee up, it's a drive," Dave explained. "When you hit a short shot, it's a chip. Golf has its own language, like baseball. Come on. Let's hit a few."

There was a bucket full of golf balls next to the cage, and a piece of carpet with a tiny little rubber thing sticking up out of it on the right side. Derek realized this must be what a golf tee looked like.

Leaning against a board on the side of the net were about seven golf clubs, each with a different face. Some were big and fat, others slimmer, shaped more like blades.

Dave took the longest, fattest-headed club and showed it to Derek. "This is a driver," he said. "You use a different club for every different kind of golf shot. That's why golfers carry around such big bags of clubs."

He took a ball, placed it on a rubber tee, and lined himself up alongside it, placing the club behind the ball. "Stand back," he told Derek. "Safety first."

Derek backed up a few steps. He'd never really watched golf on TV. It looked totally boring, just watching balls fly and guys tapping balls into cups.

But now he watched silently and intently as Dave slowly took the club back and up, then quickly swung through the ball. There was a sharp clicking sound, and the ball smacked into the center of a padded bull's-eye that hung on the front of the cage.

"Whoa!" Derek said. "That would have gone a mile!"

Dave's golf swing looked perfect, Derek noted with amazement. It was just like the pros he'd seen swinging on TV—and was *exactly the same as Dave's baseball swing.* Now Derek understood why that swing was so long and loopy! It didn't work too well in baseball, but it was well suited for golf.

"To tell you the truth," Dave said, "I've only ever played golf. Never baseball. Not even once. I only signed up for baseball because Chase thought it would help me make friends here." He smiled. "And here you are, so I guess he was right. Anyway, I was thinking maybe you could help me with my game."

"That's why I wanted you to come over to the Hill and hang out with us."

"Yeah . . . well . . . I don't know if I'm ready for that yet.

I mean, those kids think I'm . . . I don't know what they think, actually, but it's not anything good."

"Ah, they just don't know you yet," Derek said. "You come up there with me, and I'll make sure they don't go off on you."

"Thanks."

"Anyway, my baseball swing's not as good as your golf swing."

"I don't know about that," Dave said modestly. "Hey. Want to try?"

"Sure!" Derek took the club from Dave. He lined himself up the way he'd seen Dave do it. Then he wound up and swung as hard as he could.

There was a whoosh as Derek spun himself around— but no clicking sound. Derek had missed the ball completely. It still sat there on the tee, waiting to be struck. "Whoa. How'd I miss that?" he said, amazed.

"Try keeping your eyes open next time. And don't swing so hard."

Had he shut his eyes? Maybe. He couldn't remember. But he had swung too hard.

"Let me try again," he said, lining up and taking another swing, a little less hard this time. He hit the ball, but off the end of the club, and it went into the side of the net. "Hmm. This is harder than it looks."

"You got that right," Dave said. "These clubs might be

a little long for you. My folks got them for me when I out-grew my old set."

Derek flushed. Dave was a lot taller than him. "I'm not exactly short," he said.

"Course not," Dave said quickly. "Here, let me show you a few things that might help." He told Derek to keep his head still all through the swing, and how to stay balanced and under control.

He showed him the proper grip, which was sort of like a baseball grip but different in several key ways. The left thumb, for instance, was tucked into the right palm along-side the club shaft, instead of being used to grasp the club, the way the thumb would be used with a baseball bat. And the right pinky interlocked with the left index finger.

Dave showed Derek how to take the club straight back, and pivot with his hips on the backswing. . . .

It was like a baseball swing, but different. Derek, who enjoyed any new challenge—especially if it involved sports—actually managed to hit some solid drives, in between a bunch of clunkers.

His competitive juices were flowing now. He felt sure that if he swung a club a few more times . . . just a few more . . . he could get it just right.

"How about those other clubs?" Derek asked. "Is it the same swing all the time?"

"No," Dave said. "First of all, you hit these off the carpet, not the tee. The smaller the club, the closer to the ball you stand, so the swing is even more up and down."

"Wow, you know a lot about this game!" Derek said, impressed.

Dave smiled and looked down for a long moment. "It's my dream," he said.

"What is?"

"One day I want to be on the PGA Tour," Dave said. "I want to win golf tournaments, like the Masters and the U.S. Open. I want to be as good as Jack Nicklaus, the greatest golfer ever."

"Wow," Derek said. "That's awesome, man. I hear you. You know . . ." He paused, then let out a chuckle. "Man, you're going to laugh when you hear what my dream is."

"I won't laugh," Dave said, shaking his head. "I promise you that. I owe you that much, after all."

"Huh?"

"You've been the entire welcoming committee, know what I mean?"

"I guess," said Derek. "Not for long, though. I've got lots of friends. And they're gonna like you fine, once they get to know you."

The two boys stayed there for another hour, sharing their dreams and hitting bucket after bucket of golf balls. Neither of them had ever met another kid with a big-time dream of sports stardom.

By the time Chase emerged from the house to tell Dave

it was time to start studying, Derek and Dave were real friends.

Real friends *with sore arms*. At least Derek's were.

On the way home Chase asked Derek lots of questions about his family, his grades, and his friends. They were exactly the same questions Derek's own parents would have asked Dave's mom and dad—if Derek had gone about setting this visit up the right way in the first place.

Then again, he hadn't known he was going to be ambushed and taken to Dave's house as a surprise. And he hadn't known Dave's parents wouldn't be home either—or even in the country! So Derek figured his mom and dad could scarcely blame him for anything, right?

Derek tried not to think about it. He would just have to deal with the flak when he got home. Meanwhile, he couldn't stop thinking how funny life was. Here he'd been thinking how different Dave was from everybody else he knew.

And what he'd come to find out instead was how much alike they both were—especially where it counted the most. They had shared their most cherished dreams with each other—and, before putting the golf clubs away, they'd sworn to support each other's dreams.

Wasn't that what good friends did?

Derek smiled, feeling glad he'd allowed Dave to "kidnap" him. He couldn't wait to introduce his new good friend to the rest of the guys at the Hill.

As the car pulled up in front of the Jeter family's townhouse, Derek saw Sharlee playing outside, bouncing a rubber ball off the stoop and catching it. When she saw Derek getting out of the Mercedes, her eyes widened in shock.

"Mom! Dad!" she screamed, so loud that his parents came to the window within seconds. "There's a movie star's car out here—and Derek was riding in it!"

Mr. and Mrs. Jeter were outside in seconds, but by the time they got there, the Mercedes was already disappearing down the street.

Derek could see the disappointment in their faces as soon as they turned to look at him, though Sharlee was still excited and happy. "Wow," she said. "My big brother knows a movie star!"

"Inside," said his dad, glaring at Derek.

"Now," added his mom. "We need to have a discussion."

They marched him inside and sat him down on the living room couch. "Sharlee, please go play outside for a little longer while we speak with Derek," Mr. Jeter said.

Looking disappointed, she left the house.

"I can explain," Derek said.

"Okay," Mrs. Jeter said. "Let's start at the beginning."

They listened as Derek told them what had happened and pleaded for them to understand.

"Oh, we understand," said his father. "We understand that you've broken your contract—big-time."

"What?" He'd never stopped to think whether he'd been

breaking a rule in the contract, but for the life of him, he couldn't think of which one he'd broken.

"Dot?"

"I'll go get it, Jeter." His mom went upstairs.

Derek and his dad sat there silently until Mrs. Jeter returned. "Okay," she said. "I see here that it says 'Respect Others.' Do you think it was respectful to your family not to tell us you were going off someplace, goodness knows where, and we have no way of reaching you, or knowing where you are? No phone call even?"

"But—" Derek thought he'd already explained that one to them, but he guessed they weren't buying his excuse. "Even though Dave's parents weren't there," he said, "it wasn't like I went somewhere without a responsible adult."

"That doesn't change anything," said his mom. "You should know we need to speak with any parents before you're able to go over to someone's house."

"Plus, you should never get into a car without us knowing the person driving," his dad added. "*And* you need to always check with us before changing your plans."

"What would have happened if we'd needed to reach you in an emergency? We would have had absolutely no idea how to find you."

"We need to know where you are," his dad chimed in, "and you need to be where you say you're going to be. That was a rule long before you even had a contract."

"Here's another one you've broken, old man," said Derek's mom, looking over the contract. "'Be a Role Model for Sharlee.'"

"That's right," Mr. Jeter said. "We don't want her taking after you and running off without telling us where she's going."

Suddenly Derek could see just how wrong he'd been. He should have told Dave right away that his family rules didn't permit surprise visits to new people's houses—not without his parents scoping out the lay of the land first. He should have thought about his contract before he went and broke it.

"I guess I didn't think about it that way," he admitted. "I thought I was making a really good new friend. I guess I just didn't see that I was also breaking my contract. I'm so sorry."

"There you go," his dad said, putting a hand on Derek's shoulder. "That's my boy."

"And we're glad you made a new friend," said his mom, "just not happy with the way you did it."

"So . . . what do I do now?" Derek asked them. "I know it was wrong, but I can't exactly take it back."

"Derek," said his mom, "I know you've kept faithfully to your contract up to now, and it's been almost a year—"

"*More* than a year," Derek corrected her.

"But there are consequences for bad behavior," his dad finished. "I know you were planning on spending the night at Vijay's this weekend, but you've just lost that privilege."

Derek looked down and nodded.

"And if you break your contract again," his mom cautioned, "we'll have to cancel those Yankees-Tigers tickets."

"No! Not that!" Derek begged.

"Maybe you'd better study this some more," his dad said, handing him the contract to look at. "You can give it back to me after you've memorized it."

"*And* after you've finished your homework," his mom said.

Derek nodded. He did have a lot of homework and studying to do. And he was going to go over his contract, too. No way he wanted to lose those Yankees-Tigers tickets!

Even more important, he never wanted to disappoint his mom and dad again.

Chapter Seven

PLAY BALL!

Derek had never felt this excited to start a new season. His Red Sox were on the field, tossing the ball around before their first game. Across the diamond Derek could see the Tigers, the team he'd been on last year—and also today's opponent.

Derek had been waiting forever since last season had ended. Since then he'd had a total of two team practices, a couple of visits to the batting cages, and a few days of pickup games at the Hill.

Today was a perfect day to start the new season. The sun was shining, the weather was warm, and the field wasn't too wet. Derek put his hands together with the rest of the Red Sox for a team cheer, then went to grab a bat. His team was up first, and he was batting third.

"Go, Derek!" he heard his mom shout, echoed a second later by Sharlee and his dad. He waved to them in the bleachers, and they waved back, clapping and whooping it up.

Cubby Katz came to the plate as all the Red Sox cheered. He stared calmly as the first pitch sailed high over his head. He stood there like a statue as the next pitch bounced at his feet. Then he stared at two more over his head.

"Take your base!" the umpire said.

Derek smiled and shook his head. Cubby was so short, it was hard to throw strikes to him. That was a huge advantage for the Sox—because Cubby was also *fast*.

On the next pitch Cubby stole second base. "Yeah!" Derek shouted from the on-deck circle.

Jason, batting second, hit a slow ground ball to the third baseman, who was playing off the bag. Jason was fast too, though not as speedy as Cubby. Jason beat the third baseman's throw to first for an infield single, and Cubby wound up on third.

Derek could barely contain his excitement. He'd been red-hot at the plate in practice. Now with two runners on, it was his big chance to start the season off right.

He took a mighty swing at the first pitch, but the ball was high, and Derek barely made contact. The result was a weak fly ball to shortstop, and the first out of the inning.

"Aaargh!" Derek groaned as he headed back to the bench. How had he missed that pitch? It had been right there in his eyes!

"That's okay, man," Dave told him as he sat back down. "You'll get 'em next time for sure."

"For sure!" Vijay agreed. "Don't worry. We're going to score now anyway. You'll see."

Derek sighed and nodded. Vijay was right. It was about what the *team* did, not about himself. He sat, watched, and cheered as Jeff, their cleanup hitter, flied to center field. Cubby tagged up and ran home after the catch, scoring the Red Sox's first run.

Isaiah came to bat next. He hit a shot down the first-base line for a double, and Jason scored to make it 2–0!

Dave came to the plate next. "Go, Dave!" Derek yelled, standing up and clapping. "Hit it out of here!"

Dave was clearly trying to do exactly that. He swung his long, loopy golf swing one, two, three times—without making any contact at all.

"Strike three!" yelled the umpire, and that was the end of the top of the inning.

Derek grabbed his mitt and trotted out onto the field, followed by the rest of the Sox. Jeff took the mound and started his warm-up throws. Jeff was usually pretty accurate. Today, though, he was all over the place. Derek guessed he was nervous.

Well, they *all* were. It was the first game of the season!

But that meant the Tigers would be nervous too, Derek thought, especially now that they were down by two runs.

But after the first hitter made it all the way to third on a sizzling ground ball up the first-base line, and the second hitter reached on a dropped fly ball in left by Miles, the Tigers had a lot fewer reasons to be nervous.

The number three hitter dug into the batter's box. Derek pounded his mitt twice with his fist. "Hit it here," he muttered. "Come on, right here . . ."

Sure enough—as if the hitter had heard him—the line drive came screaming right at Derek's head! He ducked and stuck his glove up, and the ball smacked right into the pocket!

It all happened in a moment. Derek saw the runner going from third base to home, thinking that the ball, hit so hard, would surely have gotten past the shortstop.

But it *hadn't*. And Derek's throw to third would have had him out easily—*if Dave had been at third to catch it*.

But, no. Dave (who had already admitted he didn't know all the rules of baseball) had no idea where he was supposed to be. He was standing well away from the base, cheering Derek instead of covering!

Derek winced at the missed opportunity for a double play. He told himself he'd better give Dave a crash course in baseball rules if he wanted the Sox to be a winner this year.

"Come on!" Jason yelled from second base. "Cover that bag!"

"Wake up!" Buster called from first. "Gotta look alive!"

Dave looked bewildered. "Don't worry about them," Derek told him. "Let's get these next two outs, huh?"

Dave nodded and got his head back into the game. Lucky thing too, because the next batter hit a sharp ground ball to him. Dave caught it cleanly and threw to second to get the runner for the second out.

Meanwhile, the man who'd been on third base scored the Tigers' first run, to cut the Red Sox's lead in half.

The next hitter watched three pitches go by for balls. Then, knowing the pitch would be right down the middle, he smacked it into the outfield, where it fell between Miles and Cubby for a double and the Tigers' second run.

The Tigers weren't through yet either. The next hitter managed a clean single, and the runner scored from second base to make it 3–2.

The batter after him grounded to second, ending the inning, *finally*, but the Red Sox had lost their lead, and Derek wasn't feeling so confident anymore.

After a scoreless second, Derek led off the third inning. This time he promised himself he wouldn't swing at the first pitch, no matter what. His first at bat had been over before it had even begun, and he wasn't about to let that happen again.

Sure enough, he let the first pitch go by, and groaned when he saw how easy it would have been to hit! The next pitch wasn't nearly as good, but Derek took a swing at it anyway—and *missed*.

Now the count was 0–2, and he had to swing at any pitch that was close to a strike, or risk being called out. The pitch came in outside, but close enough that Derek had to swing.

He made contact, but it wasn't solid contact. His weak pop-up was caught by the first baseman for the out, and Derek shook his head in frustration as he headed back to the bench again.

On the way he glanced up into the bleachers and saw his family trying to cheer him up. Derek raised both arms toward his dad, as if to say, *What am I doing wrong?*

His dad made a motion with both his hands palm down, as if to say, *Calm down*.

Derek nodded. It was good advice. The game was far from over, and this was no time to get down on himself.

In the bottom of the fourth, with the score still 3–2, Jeff gave up a leadoff triple. He struck out the next two batters, keeping the runner at third. But the next batter singled the run in, to make it 4–2, Tigers.

Jeff struck out the next guy to end the inning, but now the Red Sox's job was twice as hard. They had to come back from two runs down instead of one, with only two innings left to play.

Jason led off the top of the fifth. Derek and the rest of the team were all standing now, clapping and yelling encouragement—and Jason gave them something to cheer about with a line drive double to right field.

Derek came to the plate, trying to calm himself down. His heart was racing, and he could feel the cold sweat on his neck.

It was hard to be calm, because he knew he could drive in a run with a single. *In fact,* he couldn't help thinking, *a homer would tie the game.*

He'd studied the Tigers' pitcher his first two times at bat, and even though Derek had made outs, he felt like he could get to the pitcher this time.

But before the guy even threw a pitch to Derek, the Tigers coach came out and made a pitching change!

As the new pitcher warmed up, Derek studied him from the on-deck circle. The new guy didn't throw too fast, at least.

Derek came to the plate ready to swing, but the first pitch was low. He tried to stop himself, but it was too late.

"Strike one!" the umpire called.

Next, Derek swung at a pitch over the plate, but the ball had a little break on it, and he fouled it off for strike two.

The third pitch was a changeup. It came in high and slow. Derek wound up, his eyes widening, and he swung so hard, he nearly came right out of his shoes!

"Strike three!" yelled the ump.

"Nooo!" Derek moaned. He'd seen the ball perfectly— it had been right down the middle! He just hadn't been ready for a pitch that was so slow.

So far he'd gone 0 for 3 in this new season, and he hadn't even come close to a hit. Worse, he'd let down his teammates and coach, and he *knew* they'd been counting on him to lead the team in hitting.

Jeff came up next, and drew a walk. Derek clapped and said, "Attaway, Jeff!" His mood began to lift, seeing that his Red Sox were trying to mount a rally even though he'd struck out.

Then Isaiah came to the plate. Obviously thinking home run, he swung too soon and too hard at a soft, slow pitch— and struck out just like Derek had.

Now it was all up to Dave, who had already struck out twice. He let the first two pitches go by for high strikes.

If he was waiting for a low pitch, he wasn't going to get one. The Tigers' coach had obviously noticed that Dave's swing was long and looping, and the coach must have told his pitcher to keep the ball high in the zone so Dave couldn't hit it.

Dave swung at the third pitch, and actually made contact, but he just managed to foul it straight up. The catcher caught it easily for the third out, and the Red Sox failed to score in the fifth, even though they'd gotten two men on base.

As Derek was about to head out to short, Coach Kaufman came up to him and said, "You're pitching."

"Me?" Derek was surprised.

"You're my number two pitcher, kid. Go get 'em."

Derek remembered that in practice the other day, Coach had told him and Buster to be ready to pitch if necessary. Derek had just never thought it would actually happen. He'd taken so many swings in the cages yesterday that his arms were sore. If he'd thought he might be pitching, he probably would have quit sooner.

But it was too late to think about that now—he had to do his job, and do it the best he could.

He tried to concentrate on throwing the ball for strikes. He could hear the crowd cheering, his mom's voice rising over some of the others, yelling, "Go, Derek!" He got the ball over for two quick strikes, then served up a pitch right down the middle that the hitter crushed for a long triple.

Derek hung his head in frustration.

"Hang in there, Derek!" Coach Kaufman urged, clapping.

Derek knew he couldn't afford to mope about the triple he'd already given up. He stared in at Isaiah's mitt and bore down, throwing his best fastball right past the next hitter, once, twice, and three times!

The third hitter couldn't seem to catch up to Derek's fastball either, fouling off two pitches before swinging through a third strike.

One more hitter, Derek told himself, *and I'll be out of this mess.* His arm was really tired now, and he wondered if he had enough strength left to get one more hitter out. He didn't think he could throw another fastball past anyone.

But, of course, the hitter didn't know that—and that was Derek's best hope for success.

He was facing the Tigers' cleanup man—their best power hitter—and Derek fooled him on the first pitch by throwing a slow one right over the middle. The hitter's eyes got as big as saucers. He swung for all he was worth, and just barely made contact, popping it up to the infield.

Derek was just about to say "Yesss!" when he realized that the shortstop, the catcher, and the third baseman were all yelling, "I got it!"

They must have heard one another shouting too, because they all backed off, and the ball fell in between them for a single—scoring the Tigers' fifth run of the game!

Derek sank to his knees and groaned in frustration. He knew these things happened sometimes, that it was just bad luck, really. But his team couldn't afford bad luck, not when they were already down!

Derek struck out the next man on three straight change-ups. But was it already too late?

The Red Sox were down to their last licks, with the bottom of the order coming up to bat. Buster, their number seven hitter, led off with a single, but could the Red Sox's subs keep the rally going?

Rocco was next. He'd been put in for Vijay in the fifth. Rocco hadn't shown much hitting ability in practice. But now, in the clutch, he managed to sock a double down the left field line, sending Buster to third base!

Suddenly the Sox had a rally going. Rocco was followed by Reggie, who'd come in for Miles at the same time that Rocco had come in for Vijay. Reggie seemed not to want to swing, but it turned out fine for the Sox, because the pitcher wound up walking him, loading the bases with nobody out!

Now Cubby came up to bat. Derek watched and cheered, knowing that a bases-clearing double here would tie the game.

Cubby hit a hard line drive, and Derek started to yell with triumph, but it was right at the third baseman, who caught it for the first out. The runner at third had to hurry back to the bag to avoid a double play!

Jason followed with a weak grounder to the pitcher, who made sure the runner at third wasn't trying to come home, then threw to first base for out number two.

Incredibly, it all came down to Derek! He was the team's last hope.

Everyone was screaming, whether for the Sox or the Tigers. *Get a hit,* Derek told himself. *Stay calm and controlled. Just . . . get . . . a hit!*

The first pitch came in, looking very fat, very slow, and very, very hittable. Derek forgot all about staying under control. He swung so hard that he threw himself off balance and fell to the ground!

The result of his mighty swing? A pathetic dribbler to

second base. Derek was out by a mile, and so were the Red Sox, by a final score of 5–2.

Derek felt like sinking into the ground. His team had put all those men on base but had scored only two stupid runs!

And it had been mostly his own fault—or at least his as much as anyone else's.

So much for a good start to the new season. Crushed, Derek lined up with his disappointed teammates to shake hands with the victorious Tigers.

Afterward the Red Sox clapped one another on the back and said "We'll get 'em next time" and stuff like that. But none of it made Derek feel any better.

He looked into the stands for his folks, and was surprised to see his mom and dad talking to none other than *Chase*!

"Hey, look," Dave said, noticing the same thing at the same time.

Derek hoped his parents weren't giving Chase a lecture about driving their son anywhere without their permission. But as Derek and Dave got closer, he saw that the three of them were smiling and laughing like old friends. Derek's dad was patting Chase on the back and nodding, like they were sharing some old memory or something!

"Derek!" His mom called him over. "C'mere!"

Derek gave Sharlee a hug first. He always did, before greeting anyone else. She was only five, but she knew well enough whether Derek's team had won or lost, and even whether Derek had done well or not. Still, Sharlee adored him either way and always thought he was the hero of the game, no matter what had actually happened.

"Derek, we've just been talking with Mr. Bradway," his dad said. "It seems we have a lot in common."

"Did you know he was in the armed forces?" Derek's mom asked, and then turned to Dave and introduced herself. "Hello, young man. I'm Derek's mom."

"Good to meet you, ma'am," Dave said, and introduced himself to Derek's family.

"As a matter of fact," said Mr. Jeter, "Chase was in Germany at the same time we both were."

"Really? Wow!" Derek's parents had met there when they were both in the Army, way back in the day.

"Derek," his mom said, "you can go over to Dave's from now on anytime. Just as long as you let us know first."

"Yes, now that we know Mr. Bradway, and we know he's like a parent to Dave, we're fine with it," his dad agreed.

"Great!" Dave said, grinning broadly. "So, Derek, want to come over after school tomorrow?"

"Um . . . I . . ."

Derek felt a surge of panic rising inside him. He knew if he went to Dave's, they'd be swinging golf clubs again, and Derek didn't want to do any more damage to his swing than he'd already done. He suspected that the reason he'd failed to get a hit today was that he'd thrown off his swing by hitting so many golf balls the day before.

"Um . . . actually, I've gotta do a bunch of homework tomorrow afternoon . . . and studying."

Derek saw Dave's face fall into a sad expression. He hated disappointing Dave, and he knew what Dave must be thinking—that Derek didn't want to be friends with him anymore.

But that wasn't it at all!

If only he could have explained right then and there! But he didn't want to say something bad about playing golf that would hurt Dave's feelings. If he could just talk to his parents first, they'd know what to do.

But there was no time for that. Chase and Dave said good-bye to the Jeters, and they went their separate ways.

Back in the car Derek finally spoke up. "Dad?"

"Yes, Son?"

"Is it possible to ruin your baseball swing by playing golf?"

"Why? Is that what you think happened today?"

"Kind of."

Mr. Jeter glanced at Derek in the rearview mirror. "How many golf balls have you been hitting?"

"I must have hit a couple hundred yesterday. Dave's got his own driving cage."

"Hmm. Couple hundred, huh? That's a whole lot."

"Yeah, my arms were really sore."

"Well, that's probably it, then," said his dad. "Your arms

were so tired, you had to put too much of your body into your swing today. No wonder you were swinging too hard."

"So you don't think I screwed up my swing by playing golf? I mean, it's two different kinds of swings . . ."

"I don't think so," said Mr. Jeter. "You don't have to worry about that. Not at this point in your career. You just make sure you don't wear yourself out before a game. That way you can get into your rhythm and let it flow."

Derek nodded. "Thanks, Dad." Now he felt better. His dad's baseball advice was always right, and it felt right this time too. His arms had been tired. It was true. And now he felt bad about hurting Dave's feelings.

As soon as they got back home, Derek ran to the phone and dialed Dave's number.

"Hello?"

"Hi. It's me, Derek."

"Oh . . . hi."

Derek could hear it in his voice. The hurt. The sadness. "Hey, man, you want to come over here tomorrow afternoon instead? We can play some ball on the Hill."

"Huh? I thought you had so much work."

"Yeah. Well, I'm gonna do it tonight."

"Great!"

He could hear the relief in Dave's voice. He must have known Derek was fudging the truth—after all, they were in the same class, with the same work and upcoming tests—but he seemed willing not to press the issue.

"So why don't you come over here, then?" Dave asked.

Derek winced. "Listen, man, you said yourself you want to learn the rules of baseball, right?"

"Yeah, but you could teach me here, too."

"Not the same as doing it during a game, with a bunch of other guys!"

"Yeah, that's the thing. . . ."

"Don't worry about them," Derek said. "You're with me, and you're my friend now. They dis you, they're dissing me, too."

"Okay, then . . . I guess," Dave said, giving in. "You sure they'll be okay with me being there?"

"Are you kidding?" Derek said, laughing. "There's always room for one more on the Hill!"

Chapter Eight

PRACTICE MAKES PERFECT?

Derek sat in class, staring at the second hand as it wound slowly around the clock. As soon as the final bell rang, Gary Parnell was all over him.

"So? How'd you do, my friend?" He held up his own science test, with the big red 98 circled in red twice, and waited for Derek's answer.

Derek scowled and held up his own paper. It was nothing to be ashamed of—a 92—but not close to Gary's grade. Once again the king of the hill had kept his throne.

It was like this all the time, or at least it had been for the past two years. At the end of the previous school year, Derek had actually outdone Gary on one single, solitary test, but that had only made Gary study harder. Derek hadn't beaten him since.

Still, the whole competition wasn't such a bad thing. Derek hadn't scored less than 90 on any of his tests all spring. Remembering his contract, he felt satisfied that he wasn't going to break the rule about working hard and getting good grades.

"I've gotta go," Derek said, gathering his papers and stuffing them into his book bag.

"Gotta go do what? Play baseball?" Gary snorted. His contempt for sports knew no bounds.

"I think you should try it sometime," Derek told him. "It might help you stay sharp. You might even get a ninety-nine or a hundred next time."

Gary rolled his eyes and looked like he wanted to say something clever, but before he could think what to say, Derek was gone, leaving him there with his mouth open.

Derek jogged down the hall and out the front doors, looking for Dave, who'd already left the classroom. But Dave was gone.

Derek hoped he would show up at the Hill and not chicken out. But Derek didn't have to worry for long. When Derek arrived, Dave was there, waiting patiently for everyone to arrive. Across the parking lot sat the Mercedes. Chase stood next to it, polishing the shiny chrome wheels with a towel.

"Hey," Dave said, holding up his mitt. "Glad you made it so quick."

"How'd you do on the test?" Derek asked.

"Eighty-nine. You?"

"Somewhere like that," Derek said. He didn't want to get into a grades competition with Dave. He wanted to teach him to play better baseball, and to make sure the other kids accepted him as part of the group.

They started tossing the ball back and forth. Vijay showed up after a few minutes, and while he was surprised to see Dave there, he didn't seem at all upset about it.

Derek put Vijay at first and Dave at third. He sent some grounders and line drives Dave's way and called out situations, to teach Dave what to do with the ball when it came his way.

If there were a runner on third, for instance, Dave would need to check the runner back to the base on a grounder before throwing to first. If he caught a liner with the runner on third, he didn't need to throw to first. Instead he had to get to third before the runner got back to the base, but he didn't need to tag him.

"Wow, there sure are a lot of rules in baseball," Dave said, shaking his head.

"It's a lot to learn all in one session," Derek admitted. "But it's gonna help. You'll see."

Things were going well for a while—until Jeff and

Jason showed up with Isaiah. When they saw Dave there, they stopped where they were and started murmuring to one another.

Dave saw them too, and Derek could tell he was worried. "Hey," Derek told him, "chill for a minute. I'll be right back." He went over to Jeff and the others and said, "What's up, guys?"

"Do we have to let that kid play with us?" Jason asked. "He thinks he's all that."

"And he stinks at baseball too," Jeff added.

"That's why I invited him here," Derek explained. "And his name is Dave. Dave Hennum. By the way, he's not a snob either. Not even close."

"Are you telling me he's not rich?" Isaiah asked.

"No . . . but he's not a snob. You guys are the ones being snobs, if you ask me," said Derek.

"Yeah, you say that because he lets you ride in the Mercedes," Jeff said with a smirk. The others laughed, and Derek was dismayed to see Vijay there, laughing along with the rest.

That really surprised Derek. Vijay of all people should have known how Dave would feel about being left out. Derek turned and saw Dave standing there, shifting from one foot to the other, waiting for someone to include him.

"Come on, guys—at least give him a chance," Derek pleaded. "Vij?"

Vijay shrugged and looked away from Derek and to Jeff.

Jeff and Jason looked at each other and shrugged also. "Okay, I guess," Jeff said. "But only for your sake, Derek. I just hope you remember who your real friends are."

Derek glanced back at Dave, who was pretending not to notice that they were all in a huddle talking and pointing to him.

"Dave's my real friend too," Derek told him, and watched as their eyes all widened. "He's a great kid."

"If you say so," said Jason. "Okay, then. Let's play ball."

And the huddle mercifully broke up. They started playing, taking positions on the slope, where the bases were marked off by landmarks such as a shrub or a bare patch on the grass.

Derek started announcing the game as usual, and Dave started to get into the swing of things, at least in the beginning. He even threw to the right base, twice—and got mock cheers from Jeff, Jason, and Isaiah.

But when Dave came to the plate and threw the ball up into the air to hit it, he kept missing—over and over again. Derek and Vijay both tried to get him to swing level, but Dave couldn't seem to get it into his head that a baseball swing was not a golf swing.

And now the snarky comments started to come, fast and furious.

"Air ball."

"Going, going . . . missed."

"Whew, felt the wind from that one!"

Finally Dave had had enough. He picked up his mitt and walked off toward where Chase was waiting by the car.

"Hey, where you going?" Derek called after him.

"Home," Dave said without turning around. "See you."

Derek jogged after him for a few paces, but Dave just walked faster, until Derek could see that there was no point. Then Derek turned back to the others.

"You guys happy now?" he asked. "I hope you're all real proud of yourselves for driving him away."

"Aw, poor baby," Jeff mocked, waving as the Mercedes pulled away. "I guess we made the baby cry."

"He didn't cry," Derek said. "And if he did, so what? How do you think those comments made him feel?"

"You can't take the heat, get out of the kitchen," said Jason, and the others laughed, including Vijay, who still wasn't looking at Derek.

"Hey," Derek said. "So what if he's not great at baseball? Lots of kids aren't that great at it, but you don't goof on *them*. Besides, maybe he's good at other things—things you guys can't even do."

"Like what?" Isaiah asked.

"Like . . . like golf!" Derek immediately wished he hadn't said that.

"*Oooh*. Golf. Of course. The rich kids' game!" All the kids laughed at Jeff's joke, missing Derek's point completely.

"Hey, you know what? I'm going home," Derek said.

"Why? What'd we do?" Jeff asked, holding his hands out. "Come on, Jeter. Don't make such a big deal out of it."

"You want to hang with me? You've got to be all right with my friends," Derek said, staring at each of them in turn. "Besides, Dave's on our team, and we need him to play better ball."

There. At least none of them could argue with that point.

"I'm going to invite him back here again soon, and I hope he comes," Derek went on. "And if he does, we're going to make him feel welcome. All right?" He waited for their answer, but none came. "All right?"

"I guess," Jeff said, shrugging. "Sure, okay."

"Me too," said Isaiah.

"Yeah, all right," said Jason.

"Vijay?"

Vijay stared at the ground and nodded. Derek guessed that there was something else eating at him, but he couldn't figure out what that might be.

Oh well, he thought. *I guess I'll find out soon enough.*

For each game, one of the players was assigned to bring snacks and drinks, and today was Derek's turn. He and his mom had brought carrots, orange slices, bananas, and juice boxes.

"That should hold 'em," said Mrs. Jeter. "Power food. You guys are going to score a lot of runs today!"

"If only it were that easy," said Derek sadly.

"Hey, old man, what's the matter?" His mom could always tell when something was on his mind. "Where's your fighting spirit today?"

Derek sighed. "Aw, Mom, the guys are ganging up against Dave, and I'm caught right in the middle."

"Well, that's the place to be, if you want to solve the problem. You just tell the guys to ease up. Dave's their teammate, for goodness' sake."

"I told them," Derek said. "But it doesn't seem to help."

"Hmm. . . . Well, my advice is, concentrate on your own game right now. Maybe the others will pick up on your focus and you guys can win the game. That'll put everybody in a more friendly mood."

Derek smiled and nodded. His mom was always full of good advice.

The kids started arriving, and soon Derek was fully involved in warm-ups. Dave showed up for the game, much to Derek's relief. He'd been afraid that after what had happened on the Hill yesterday afternoon, Dave might just drop out of Little League altogether!

But Dave seemed to have a fighting spirit much like Derek's. He might have given up on making friends with the other guys, but he hadn't given up on baseball. He seemed focused and ready, even if he didn't say much to anyone but Derek.

"How's it goin'?" Derek asked him.

"I'm all right," Dave assured him. "I'm gonna hit one out today, and show those guys."

"Attaboy," Derek said. "Me too."

They high-fived, just as the umpire yelled, "Play ball!"

Today they were facing the Yankees, the team Derek had always wanted to be a part of—even in Little League.

The Yankees' pitcher started out wild, walking Cubby and Jason. Derek came to the plate with two men on and nobody out. He was psyched!

In fact, he was so excited about driving those two runs in that he struck out swinging. He returned to the bench, furious with himself. He'd overswung at every pitch. He promised himself not to do that again next time up.

Luckily, the Yankees' pitcher was so wild that he walked three runs in before the coach came in and made a substitution. Derek felt bad for the kid, but he was happy his team was up 3–0.

Unluckily, the new pitcher threw strike after strike, mowing down Vijay and Miles to end the inning.

Worse, in the bottom of the first, the Yankees took the lead. Coach Kaufman had started Buster instead of Jeff at pitcher, not because Jeff had pitched the game before but because Coach Kaufman wanted to give other kids a chance at key positions.

But there was a downside to Coach Kaufman's good-heartedness. Buster didn't have Jeff's accurate arm, or Derek's power fastball, and the Yankees torched him for four runs in the first inning.

After that the game settled down. Nobody on the Red Sox was hitting, even though they were putting runners on base via the walk.

Derek kept coming up with men on base. Maybe because of that, he kept getting too excited—swinging too hard, or too late, or at pitches that were wide of the plate, or in the dirt, or over his head.

He was lunging and jumping at the ball, and he struck out twice more, missing big chances for RBIs.

Late in the game, standing at shortstop, he found himself thinking about his at bats so far. He was 0 for 7 already! He'd never hit so poorly in his life, and he didn't know how to handle it.

Coach Kaufman was a nice guy, but he didn't seem to know many of the fine points of the game, let alone Derek's swing. There wasn't going to be any help from that direction. Derek wished his dad were his coach, so he could give Derek some quick pointers that would help fix his swing.

By the sixth inning the score was 6–3 Yankees, and time was running out for the Sox. Derek stood in the on-deck circle with one out and two men on, and watched as Jason came through with a clutch single that scored the Sox's fourth run.

Okay, Derek told himself, trying to think what advice his

dad would have given him in this situation. *Stay calm . . . stay back . . . swing at strikes.*

There was so much to keep straight in his head! When you were the go-ahead run at the plate, it was hard to keep from overswinging—but Derek was determined to make solid contact this time around.

He let two pitches go by, just to calm himself down. Then, with the count 1–1, the pitcher threw a curveball.

It should have been easy to hit, but Derek hadn't been expecting it. He tried to stay back, but his bat hit slightly over the ball, and he grounded right back to the pitcher, who started an easy double play to end the game.

Derek sank to his knees and put his head in both hands. How could he have messed up so badly? Now his team was 0–2. And worst of all, he'd played two games and hadn't gotten even one hit yet!

Chapter Nine

THE SWING DOCTOR

After shaking hands with the winning team, Derek looked for his parents in the stands. There they were, with Sharlee standing close to their mom, looking sad.

He hugged her but avoided her hurt-looking gaze, focusing instead on his father. "Dad," he said with a pleading note in his voice, "will you take me to the batting cages after school tomorrow?"

"Hmm . . ." Mr. Jeter seemed to be thinking it over. "Tell me, Derek, how'd you do on that science test?"

"I got a ninety-two," Derek said. "It was hard, too!"

"All right, all right," Mr. Jeter said with a smile. "I guess ninety-two isn't so bad."

"Yessss!"

"How about you invite your new friend?" Mr. Jeter suggested. "And Vijay, too. Maybe they'd like to come along."

"Sure!" Derek said excitedly, turning to see where Dave and Vijay were. Dave was alone at the end of the team bench and was about to leave. Derek knew the Mercedes would be around the corner, where no one could see it or connect it to Dave.

Derek felt sorry for him. Dave didn't want anyone to know he was rich, but really, it was way too late for that. He'd have been better off just being who he was and giving the kids time to get to know him.

"Dave!" he called.

"Hey," said Dave, looking as defeated as the rest of the Red Sox.

"Want to come with me and my dad to the batting cages? He's great at fixing swings."

"Sure! I could really use some work on mine!" Dave's face brightened hopefully. "When?"

"After school tomorrow?"

"Great! I'll just ask Chase, but I'm sure it'll be okay. Meet you there?"

"Cool." They high-fived, and Derek turned to find Vijay, who was standing with a bunch of the other kids, talking in low voices and glancing over at Dave, who was already walking away.

"Hey, Vij, want to come to the cages with me and my dad after school tomorrow? We can drive you."

"Sure!" Vijay said instantly. "Definitely yes!"

"Dave's going to come too, probably," Derek added.

Suddenly Vijay's expression changed. "Oh," he said, looking away, over at the other kids nearby. It was almost like he wanted to make sure they weren't listening. "Well . . . um, okay," he said in a hushed voice. "Never mind the lift, though. I'll ask my parents to drop me there."

"Cool."

Derek was confused. What was up with Vijay? It was the strangest thing—and it seemed to be connected to Dave. . . .

Whatever it was, Derek hoped it went away fast. Like, before their batting session the next afternoon.

Dave leaned back on his right foot, waiting for the ball machine to fling its next missile his way. When the ball shot out of the chute, he made sure to keep his swing level all the way through the strike zone.

"There you go! That's right, like you're chopping down a tree. Good! Swing down at it. Yeah. You see how you hit that one?"

Derek's dad clapped his hands and patted Dave on the back as he left the cage and handed the bat to Derek. The three boys were taking turns being coached by Mr. Jeter while Chase looked on, silently observing.

Meanwhile, Derek's mom and Vijay's parents stood watching from a distance, talking and drinking coffee from wax paper cups. Sharlee had a Slurpee, and was trying to eat it before it melted all over her.

"Your swing is getting long, Derek," his dad said. "Get your weight on your back foot more—that's it."

Derek was a hard worker when it came to most things, but he never worked harder than when he was in the batting cages. He would take as many swings as his dad would let him, even if his arms felt like they were falling off.

After several turns, each lasting twenty swings, Derek was hitting nearly every ball solidly, thanks to his dad's expert tips. He felt more and more confident that come next game, he would break out of his 0 for 8 slump and start hitting like the player he knew he was.

While Vijay took his last turn, Dave said to Derek, "Your dad is an awesome coach."

"Yeah," Derek agreed with a sigh. "I only wish he would finally coach me sometime."

"What do you mean? He's coaching us right now," Dave pointed out.

It was true. Derek realized he was lucky to have a dad who cared enough to take time out of his busy day to help him improve his skills.

Still . . .

"I mean coach my *team*," Derek said.

"You really *should* be a coach, Mr. Jeter," Vijay piped up. "Did you guys see me just now? I smashed that ball!"

"You boys know I'm in school," said Derek's dad. "And you all know school comes first. When I finish my degree, we'll see."

"Dad!" Derek cried, alarmed. "What do you mean, 'we'll see'?"

"Mind your contract, Derek," said his dad, giving him a smile and a wink.

Chase came over and clapped Dave and Derek on the shoulders. "You're a natural athlete, young man," he said to Derek. "Ever think of taking up golf? You'd be good at it, you know."

"Oh. Thanks," Derek said. "Maybe after baseball season is over . . ."

"By the way, I noticed a little hitch in your swing. You might want to keep an eye on it."

"Huh? Oh! Okay." Until that moment Derek hadn't had the slightest idea that Chase knew a thing about baseball. That man was full of surprises!

At that moment Jeff and Jason stepped out of a car that had just parked in the lot. They saw Derek, Dave, and Vijay, and waved.

Derek noticed that Vijay ran right over and high-fived them. The three boys stood near the shed where the cashier sold the tokens for the machines, huddling and talking, glancing over at Derek and Dave every now and then.

Derek shook his head. Vijay was acting weird again,

but it was too late to find out why. Chase and Dave were already walking over to the Mercedes, and Derek's parents were waiting by the station wagon. As he walked over to them, Derek caught Vijay's voice.

"I just happened to run into them here . . . ," he heard his friend say.

More troubled than ever, Derek got into the car for the short ride home.

"Hey, old man," his mom said cheerfully over her shoulder from the front seat. "You looked good up there."

"Yeah, I felt good," Derek said. "Thanks to Dad."

"You're welcome," said Mr. Jeter. "You and your friends all made some nice improvements."

"You guys seem like the Three Musketeers, you were having so much fun together," said Mrs. Jeter.

"Yeah," said Derek. "Till the end, when Jeff and Jason showed up."

"Oh? What happened then?"

Derek clucked his tongue. "Vijay started acting weird. It's like, he's cool as long as it's just me and him and Dave. But as soon as someone else comes around, he's laughing and joking with them, and I know they're making fun of Dave."

"What?" his mom said, surprised. "Really? Why would anyone make fun of Dave?"

"Because he's new, and he's super rich, and he has a huge Mercedes with a driver, and lives in a mansion, and—"

"Okay, okay, I get it," said Mrs. Jeter. "Well, maybe you

should have a talk with Vijay about it. Tell him how you feel."

"I don't know. . . ."

"Hey, Derek," said his dad. "We're proud of you for the way you went and made friends with someone who didn't have any friends yet. You made Dave feel welcome, and that's a good thing."

"Funny that Vijay wouldn't understand that," Mrs. Jeter said. "I remember when their family first came here."

"I *will* talk to him," Derek decided.

That was the easy part. The hard part was figuring out what to say, and how to say it.

Soon it was time for dinner, and it was one of the quietest dinners the Jeter family had had in a long while. Normally there was lots of conversation and plenty of laughter. But tonight Derek was subdued, playing with his chicken parm more than eating it.

Even stranger, Sharlee was almost totally silent. "Yes, please," "No thank you," and "I don't know," were all she would say.

"What's wrong, Sharlee? Don't you feel well?" Mrs. Jeter asked worriedly.

"I don't know," she said, pushing her food around the plate with her fork.

"Are you sick? Is something bothering you?" Mr. Jeter wondered.

"I'm not hungry. May I be excused?"

Mrs. Jeter felt Sharlee's forehead. "I'm not sick! I told you," said Sharlee.

"No fever," Mrs. Jeter said to her husband. "Well, Sharlee, if there's anything on your mind, you know—"

"I'm tired," Sharlee said. "I want to go up to bed."

"What?" Derek said, his eyes wide. He never thought he'd ever hear those words come out of his sister's mouth.

Sharlee, however, was already halfway up the stairs. "Something's on her mind," Mrs. Jeter said. "I should go up and talk to her."

"Wait a while, Dot," Mr. Jeter advised. "She'll come out with it herself when she's ready."

"I'll go talk to her," Derek said. "Soon as I finish dessert."

Mrs. Jeter bent over him and kissed him on top of the head. "That's a good big brother," she said.

But by the time Derek had finished his chocolate chip cookie, washed up, and put his pajamas on, Sharlee was already fast asleep.

Derek frowned. He agreed with his parents. Something was definitely up with Sharlee—something she didn't want to talk about but serious enough to ruin her usual good mood.

Oh well, he thought. It would have to wait till morning, or till the next time he got to talk to her alone.

Anyway, what could be so bad at five years old?

Dimly he remembered what it was like to be five, when

any little thing could get you upset. Yeah, this was probably a big nothing. Nothing as complicated as his own
problem with Vijay, or his problems at the plate.

As he lay in bed, staring up at the ceiling in the dark-
ness, he tried one last time to guess what could be bothering his sister.

And as he fell asleep, a memory flashed before his
eyes—the memory of the Jeter family on the local basketball court, and of a couple of boys passing by . . .

Sharlee's mood had taken a dive then, too. Derek wondered if there could possibly be a connection. . . .

And then he fell asleep.

Chapter Ten

GAME ON!

On Saturday, Derek arrived at Westwood Fields early, as he always did. He liked being the first one there. It gave him more time to warm up, practice throwing and catching, and get his head into the upcoming game.

It was especially important today. Derek was concentrating hard, trying to hold on to all the adjustments he'd made under his father's guidance the day before.

He'd felt sure yesterday that his hitting would improve. But now he was starting to wonder. It had been a whole twelve hours since then. What if he'd lost the groove he'd been in?

But all of those thoughts left his head when he got to the field and saw that Dave was already there—and in a total panic.

"I can't believe this!" he told Derek. "My parents found out it was my turn to bring snacks for the team, so Mom's assistant called a gourmet catering company, and they sent over all of these crazy snacks. I mean, look at this mess!"

Derek looked. He didn't see a mess. Not at all. What he saw, instead of the usual orange slices, plain popcorn, raisins, and cooler of ice water, was a luxurious spread of foods from some local gourmet market.

There were little sandwiches with the crusts cut off the bread and toothpicks stuck into them, all wrapped in multicolored plastic. He saw three different kinds of popcorn, none of them plain, all of them dolled up with some fancy coating or other. One was marked "truffle oil," something Derek had never even heard of. There were organic fruit juices, and there was a platter of raw vegetables all cut and placed neatly around a bowl of dip.

"This looks pretty good," he offered.

"Are you kidding me?" Dave moaned. "Everyone's gonna laugh their heads off about me being a brat. They already hate me for it!"

"Aw, come on, man. Nobody *hates* you. . . ."

Derek realized he wasn't getting through when Dave started ripping the nice plastic wrap and ribbon ties off the trays. "Chase went to the grocery store to get normal stuff," he said. "But he'll never get back here in time." He sighed and grasped his head in both hands.

"Come on. Let's get to work," Derek told him, dropping his mitt and helping Dave get rid of at least the most obvious signs of luxury in the spread of food.

By the time the other kids started arriving, things didn't look quite so flashy. The toothpicks were gone, the ribbons and plastic wrapping had disappeared into a nearby trash can, the cards naming the three kinds of popcorn were gone, and the wood-shaving confetti underneath it all had been disposed of the same way.

"Hey, looks good!" said Jason as he surveyed the snack table. Tasting the popcorn with truffle oil, he added, "Outstanding. Hey, Hennum, what's this made with? It's pretty good."

Other kids heard him, and soon they were all devouring the snacks.

"Whew," Dave said, pretending to wipe sweat off his brow and shooting Derek a secret smile. "Just made it!"

As he said that, they both spotted Chase coming down the street with two huge shopping bags full of snack food. "No!" Dave mouthed, waving his hands for Chase to turn around and get lost before he gave away the whole thing.

Chase seemed confused at first, but then, seeing all the kids surrounding and devouring the existing snacks, he smiled and turned around, heading back to where the Mercedes was parked around the corner.

Warm-ups followed, and soon it was game time. The Red Sox were 0–2, and Derek was 0 for 8 at the plate, but he felt sure that today would be different—and better.

Their opponents, the Mets, were 1–1 so far, and they came to bat first.

From the moment the first pitch left Jeff's hand, Derek was totally into the game. He shouted encouragement as Jeff mowed down two Mets hitters. Then Derek lunged to his left to stop a sharp ground ball, and fired to first, just nipping the runner for the third out.

"Attaboy, Derek!" Coach Kaufman yelled, high-fiving Derek as he returned to the bench. "Way to snag it!"

"Thanks," Derek said, giving his coach a quick thumbs-up before grabbing a bat and getting ready for his first turn at the plate.

Cubby started the Sox off with a dribbler that turned into a single. Then he stole second. With one out Derek came to the plate, ready to put his newfound hitting confidence to the test.

His father had reminded him to "swing at strikes." It sounded obvious, but when you were at the plate, anxious to drive that run in from second, it was hard to hold back. You might think you were going to hit it a mile, but if it wasn't in the right hitting zone, you would succeed only in getting yourself out.

Derek waited, letting the count go to 2–1. Then, seeing the next pitch, a fastball, come right down the middle, he let it rip.

Crack! The ball screamed right back at the pitcher, who ducked to save his life—or at least his face.

But because Cubby was at second, the second baseman was playing close to the bag, and Derek's hot shot came right to him. The second baseman snagged it and stepped on the bag before Cubby could get back there.

Double play!

Derek looked up at the sky and groaned. He'd hit the stuffing out of that one! Yet all he'd gotten for his success were two outs for his team, and a snuffed-out rally.

Jeff had started the game as pitcher, but he was on a short pitch limit because the league rules said you couldn't overuse one pitcher, for fear of hurting their arm.

Derek wondered if Coach would make Derek pitch again, like he had in the first game. Derek had done okay that time, but he didn't want to pitch. He wanted to be here, at shortstop!

The Red Sox scored twice in the second inning, with Vijay knocking in both runs with a scorching double down the first-base line!

"Yeaaah!" Derek screamed, applauding his friend.

For his part, Vijay was so excited that he kept jumping up and down, his hands skyward, until Coach Kaufman reminded him to keep his head in the game.

Then Dave came up to the plate, hitting eighth because he'd done so poorly up till now in the sixth spot. Derek had been afraid Coach would demote *him* in the batting order too, but it hadn't happened, at least not today.

Dave let two high strikes go by. Then the pitcher tried throwing one in the dirt.

Big mistake. Dave's beautiful golf swing met the ball an inch above the ground and sent it soaring to left field, where it landed ten yards behind the outfielder. By the time he'd caught up to it and thrown it back in, Dave was stomping on home plate with his first home run—and RBIs—of the season!

"Your dad is *the man*!" Dave told Derek. "Did you see that?"

"Yeah, man. And so did he!" Derek answered, pointing to his dad in the stands. Dave raised a triumphant clenched fist in Mr. Jeter's direction, and Derek saw that his dad was beaming with pride, applauding.

In the third inning, with the score still 4–0, Derek got his second turn at bat. This time there was one man on and nobody out. All he needed to do was advance the runner, but Derek wanted badly to do more—much more!

In spite of all the good advice his dad had given him, he swung too hard and popped up to short for the first out.

Derek wanted to slam his bat onto home plate, but he knew that would be bad sportsmanship. It would also show disrespect for the game, and disrespect definitely was banned by his contract.

So he kept his temper and walked slowly, silently back to the bench.

"You'll get 'em next time, kiddo," said Coach Kaufman, clapping him encouragingly on the back.

But Derek wasn't so sure. His dad's coaching had helped his friends a lot, but he couldn't see that it had done anything for him at all.

Luckily, the Sox continued to score runs without his help. Before the inning was over, it was 6–0, thanks to another extra-base hit by none other than Vijay. "Oh yes!" he cried from third base, doing a little happy dance on the bag. "Ooooh yes, oh yes, oh yes, yes, yes!"

Derek laughed. Good old Vijay. No matter how down Derek felt, Vijay could always snap him out of it by being his silly, free-spirited self.

Dave proceeded to single Vijay in for the team's seventh run. When the inning finally ended, Dave was surrounded and congratulated by everyone on the team.

Derek shook his head, smiling. Suddenly everyone was Dave's good buddy. There was nothing like winning to make friends out of strangers, he thought. Just like his mom had said.

In the fourth inning Coach Kaufman moved Jeff to first and put Buster in as pitcher. The Mets, who hadn't even made good contact against Jeff all game, must have been glad to see him leave the mound. They started hitting Murph right away. Before the Red Sox knew it, they saw their big lead cut to 7–4.

With the bases loaded and only one man out, Coach

Kaufman came out and made another switch, this time handing the ball to Derek.

It was exactly what he'd been afraid of, but Derek knew he had to stay positive and just be the best pitcher he could be.

He threw the first pitch as hard as he could, right over the heart of the plate. The hitter was ready for it, though, and smashed it right back at him.

Somehow—whether it was instinct, athletic ability, or just plain luck—Derek stuck his glove out to protect his head, and the ball smacked right into the pocket!

Realizing he had the runner stranded off first base, Derek threw there to complete the double play and end the inning. Amazingly, it was exactly the same kind of double play he'd hit into himself, back in the first inning.

Everyone on the Sox roared with triumph. "What a catch!" Coach Kaufman yelled. "Did you see that?" he asked no one in particular.

Derek breathed a sigh of relief. He knew he'd been lucky. That ball could just as easily have knocked his head off. Still, he felt better having done something to contribute to the team's effort.

That good feeling didn't last long, though. Derek struck out in the fourth and felt like he was going to explode in frustration. It took a supreme effort to keep his cool and not melt down in front of everybody.

The game continued, with the Red Sox scoring three

more runs in the fifth. Derek could have been a big part of it—he came to bat with two more men on base—but in spite of the fact that he stayed calm, swung at strikes, and kept his swing level, he wound up hitting only a long fly ball that was run down by the center fielder for an out.

The runner at third did come home, for Derek's first RBI of the season, but that didn't make him feel much better. Three games, and he still didn't have a single hit! His batting average was still a big fat .000.

Still, the Sox had a 10–4 lead with just half an inning to go. Derek's arm was sore and tired, and he allowed two runs to score in the top of the sixth, but in the end he managed to seal the Red Sox's first victory of the season with a pair of strikeouts.

Derek joined in the team's raucous celebration at the mound. He was happy his team had won, happy for Vijay and Dave—but as for his own performance, he couldn't help feeling terribly disappointed.

"Hey, come on now," his dad said when Derek came over to greet his family. "Why the long face?"

"What do you mean?" Derek said. "I stunk. Again."

"Don't say that!" his mom jumped in. "How are you going to get out of your slump if you keep thinking negative thoughts?"

"Exactly," said his dad. "Instead of thinking how badly you did, look at the bright side."

"What bright side?" Derek asked. "That we won? Okay, I'm glad about that. But I still stunk."

"Nonsense!" said his mom. "You played great in the field, and you hit the ball hard almost every time. You just got unlucky a couple times. But you got an RBI."

"You didn't pitch too badly either," his dad added.

"I gave up two runs."

"You struck out five guys," his dad said. "And both those two runs came on that one home run."

"Hey, old man, keep your chin up," said his mom. "Take this win and build on it."

"That's right," said his dad. "You keep swinging like that, and just be patient. Bad luck tends to even out over time. Next time you might be as lucky as you were unlucky today. The main thing is to be consistent with your approach. Don't get too high or too low."

"All right, Jeter," his mom told his dad. "Derek's had enough coaching for one day. He's got a lot to digest. Speaking of which—it's time to go home and have dinner."

Derek knew they were right, but he still didn't feel very good about his performance. He was quiet on the way home in the car—and so was Sharlee. In fact, she had hardly said a word the whole time.

He thought back to the other night, when she'd seemed so down and he'd promised his parents he'd talk to her.

Well, he hadn't—not yet. Derek promised himself to

look for the right moment to approach her about it.

Sharlee didn't like talking about her problems any more than he did, so he had to pick his moment carefully. But he was determined to get to the bottom of what was bothering her. Stewing about things was no good, he knew that from his own experience. Only talking things out made it any better.

Chapter Eleven

PATIENCE PAYS OFF

Derek spent the next Monday in school trying not to think about all the important things on his mind. It was important to pay attention, he knew. All this stuff they were studying now would be on their finals in June.

Gary didn't make it any easier with his constant whispered taunts. "Nice doodles," he commented now, as Derek tried to cover up the drawings he'd been idly making while only half-listening to the math review.

Derek had been thinking of all kinds of things—his hitting slump, for one. But most of all, his mind had been on Sharlee, whom he *still* had not asked about what was bothering her.

He could have asked her the night before, he knew, but

she hadn't seemed too bummed out at that moment.

Still, she hadn't been her old bubbly self for at least two weeks, and he knew he would have to make her tell him what was on her mind the very next time he saw her.

But none of these thoughts were supposed to be on his mind *in class*.

"Maybe you should take up art instead of sports," Gary suggested with a snigger.

Derek gritted his teeth but didn't answer back. He knew it would only get him in trouble with Mr. Beckham, and more trouble was the last thing he needed—especially considering the warning his parents had given him about violating his contract again.

He was glad he had that contract, come to think of it, or he might have gotten himself into trouble with a rash reaction just now. Still, he was glad—and relieved—when the bell rang. Grabbing his book bag, he rushed out of there, determined to get home and over to Westwood Fields as soon as possible.

As usual, Derek got to the field before any of his teammates. Westwood Fields weren't that far away from Mount Royal Townhouses—just a five-minute drive—and one or both of his parents always made themselves available to drive him to practices and games, and to stay to cheer him on.

Today it was his dad. Sharlee had a kickball tournament

at her kindergarten, and their mom had gone with her.

Derek knew Sharlee would be disappointed that he and his dad weren't there to see her play in her first sports tournament. But in the Jeter family everyone's events were equally important. Even Sharlee would understand that Derek's game meant as much to him as her kickball match did to her.

"Now, remember," his dad counseled as Derek got out of the car, "just try to make solid contact; stay level and in control. Positive thoughts only, right?"

"Right!" Derek chirped, and headed toward the diamond where his game would soon begin.

As his teammates arrived, Derek noticed that they were in a more hopeful mood than usual. Clearly the Red Sox's recent victory, their first, had changed the atmosphere. Today's opponent, the Angels, were 3–0, though. It would not be easy to beat them and keep the victory train rolling.

Derek's mind was especially focused on his own hitting slump. Would today be the day he broke out of it? On the way to the game, his dad had reminded him about how hard he'd hit the ball in the last game, even though Derek was still without a hit for the season.

Still, as he came to the plate in the first with two men on, his heart was racing and pounding hard inside his chest. "Steady . . . ," he muttered to himself. "Stea . . . dy. . . ."

WHACK!

The ball rose over the second baseman's head and

was still rising, a long line drive, as it went over the right fielder's head. Derek's heart leapt with excitement, and he took off as fast as he could run. He was already around second base by the time the throw came back in, and he slid into third with a ringing triple—and two runs batted in!

"Yesss! Finally!" he shouted, thrusting both fists into the air.

"Yeah, Derek!" He heard his father shouting himself hoarse to be heard above everyone else's cheers. "That's the stuff!"

Clapping his hands together, Derek got his head right back into the game. Jeff, batting behind him, hit a ground ball to short, and Derek was off to the races. He slid into home plate a second ahead of the tag. "Safe!" yelled the umpire, and the Sox led 3–0.

Before the first inning was over, they scored five runs, thanks to a two-run homer by Dave, who was back in the number six spot in the order. This time, Dave clobbered a pitch that was only at his knees, not in the dirt.

Jeff came around to score ahead of him, and as Dave rounded third, he pointed at Mr. Jeter and tipped his cap, thanking him for the coaching he'd given him at the batting cages.

"Hey, Jack Nicklaus strikes!" Jeff yelled as he high-fived Dave, along with all the others. "Yeah, Jack! Way to go!"

Derek grinned and shook his head. It seemed Dave had

a bunch of new friends, and even a new nickname. Derek hoped it would stay like that the next time Dave struck out or made an error in the field.

But it was hard to feel too bad about anything at the moment. With his team up 5–0, and his epic slump at an end, Derek now focused on making up for lost time at the plate.

All game long he feasted on the Angels' pitching, going 5 for 5 with four RBIs. Vijay had a single and a double, Dave didn't strike out even once, and the team wound up winning their second straight game—by a score of 12–3— against the previously undefeated Angels!

Derek and his dad chatted all the way home about the game, hitting, slumps, staying consistent, and not getting down on yourself.

By the time they got home, Derek was feeling really good. He was in the best mood he'd been in since the season had started.

But when they went inside, his mom wasn't smiling. "Something's definitely up with Sharlee," she told them.

"Kickball game go okay?" asked Mr. Jeter.

"It went totally fine," said Mrs. Jeter. "And she was great too. She kicked in the winning run, and her team won. But after . . ."

"What?" Derek asked.

"I don't know," his mom said. "She was jumping up and

down with the other kids, and I turned away for a minute to talk to some of the parents, and when she came over to me, she was practically crying."

"She wouldn't say why?" Mr. Jeter asked, frowning.

"No. Not to me, anyway. I couldn't get it out of her. You know how stubborn she can be when she sets her mind to something."

"Is she in her room?" Derek's dad asked. "I'll go talk to her."

"No, let me," Derek said. "I'll get it out of her, I promise."

His parents looked at each other, then nodded to him. Derek went up the stairs and into Sharlee's room. His sister was lying facedown on her bed, and Derek thought she might even be crying. "Hey," he said. "What's up?"

She flailed one arm his way, indicating that he should leave the room. He didn't. "What, you don't want to talk about it?"

She made a sound that was muffled by the sheets but that clearly meant "no."

"Tell you what," he said. "I'm just going to sit here on your bed right next to you until you feel like talking about it."

"I'm never going to talk about it!" she said, suddenly rolling over and sitting up. Her face was tear-stained, and Derek wanted to hug her, but he could see she wouldn't take it well at the moment.

"I heard you had a great kickball game," he said. "Sorry I missed it."

"I'm never playing kickball again!" she said, and threw herself back down onto the bed, facedown.

"Come on, Sharlee," Derek pleaded. Then a thought crossed his mind—a memory, really. "Hey," he said. "It doesn't have anything to do with that kid, does it?"

She sat up again. "What kid?"

"The big kid who was at the basketball court the other week, around when I had my first baseball practice. I remember you were close to crying then, too."

"I'm not crying!" she said, tears welling in her eyes.

"Hey," Derek said. "It *is* about him, isn't it?"

She was silent, looking down at her lap.

"You see? I guessed. So why don't you tell me what's going on?"

She sniffed. "You can't tell Mom and Dad—*ever*!"

"Okay," he said. "Why not?"

"Because! Just promise you won't!"

"Why, because you're embarrassed?"

"Yesssssss!"

"Okay, okay," Derek said. "I promise. Now tell me."

"It's Jimmy Vickers. He's so mean to me! When I scored the winning run today, he called me bad names and said the other kids were letting me score because I'm a girl!"

"Sharlee, what do you care?" Derek said. "He's just jealous. You scored the winning run, right?"

"So? I've scored a lot of goals."

"Great. I know you're a good athlete. Jimmy just

doesn't like it that a girl plays better than he does. That's his problem."

"But Jimmy told all the boys not to let me play any-more!" Sharlee wailed, tears erupting from her eyes. "And last week he tripped me. See where my knee is all scratched? Everyone was laughing at me! *And* this morning he spit on me!" Throwing herself into Derek's arms, she sobbed bitterly.

Derek was steaming now. *I'm going to teach that kid a lesson,* he told himself. *He's going to be sorry he ever messed with my little sister.*

"Don't worry, Sharlee," he told her. "I'm going to take care of this. First thing tomorrow."

Sharlee picked up her head, staring at him with hope in her eyes. "What are you going to do?"

"I said I'll take care of it," Derek said. And he meant it. Never in his life had he felt so angry. "I promise you, you're not going to have any more problems with Jimmy."

"Oh, Derek," Sharlee said, hugging him tightly as she beamed with love and happiness. "You're the best brother ever!"

Chapter Twelve

PUSH COMES TO SHOVE

All the next day Derek waited for his moment. There was no chance at recess. The kindergartners took their break earlier than the older kids. So he waited, knowing that after school all the kids lined up outside by the buses that would take them home.

His fury had not gone away. How dare that punk pick on his little sister, the sweetest little girl in the world! Derek was going to teach him a lesson that he wouldn't forget.

At the same time there was a little nagging voice in the back of his head telling him not to go through with it, that he was going to regret it. But Derek didn't listen to that voice, because if he did, it would mean not taking action.

He'd already let Sharlee down by not finding out the

cause of her problem when he'd first noticed she was unhappy—weeks ago, back on the basketball court. He knew he should have been more alert to her needs and not waited so long to talk to her when he'd known something had to be wrong. He was her big brother, after all— her hero!

How had he let things get this far?

At any rate he had no intention of letting them go any further, little nagging voice or no. After school he waited outside by the buses with his friends, until he spotted Jimmy Vickers coming out the school doors. Then he made his move, following Jimmy onto his bus.

His hands grabbed Jimmy's shirtfront before the kid even knew what was happening, and Derek shoved him down onto the seat.

Jimmy might have been in kindergarten, and Derek in fourth grade, but they couldn't have been ten pounds apart in weight. Jimmy was a really big kid, so big that it was easy for Derek to forget the difference in their ages.

Derek thrust his finger into Jimmy's face and said, in a low, growling voice, "Now who's scared? Huh? You think you can pick on anybody you want and get away with it? How dare you spit on Sharlee? That's my little sister, okay? If you ever do anything again to hurt her—or her feelings—you'll be sorry!"

Jimmy burst into tears and started wailing. Derek's parents had always told him that all bullies were really cowards, and Jimmy was surely no different. And he was only a little kid. Derek must have seemed really scary in his fury.

Derek became vaguely aware of the astonished kids around him, staring at the spectacle. An instant later the strong hand of Mr. Lopez, the dean of the school, grabbed him, yanked him away from Jimmy, and pulled him back off the bus.

Standing at the curbside, Derek saw that half the school was staring at him, openmouthed.

"What in the world were you thinking!" Mr. Lopez asked Derek. But he wasn't really waiting for an answer. Not right then. "You're coming with me to the principal's office, young man," he said.

Inside the office Mr. Lopez directed him to a chair. "Sit there, and not a word out of you until Mr. Merckling gets here," he said before leaving.

Tears sprang to Derek's eyes, and he wiped them away furiously. Why should he feel ashamed? he asked himself. He'd only been sticking up for his little sister, like any big brother should!

But even as he thought that, he knew that everyone else might not see it quite that way. A fourth grader yelling at and threatening a kindergartner? Suddenly Derek saw that he had gotten himself into a whole world of trouble.

Part of him already felt bad about what he'd done—the part represented by that nagging little voice in his head, the voice he hadn't listened to. And Derek knew that even worse was to come.

Mr. Merckling, the principal, came in, sat down, picked up the telephone, and dialed a number. "Hello, Mrs. Jeter?"

Oh no! Derek could not have imagined a worse thing happening! He knew instantly that his parents would not be pleased about his behavior.

"Your son, Derek, is in my office . . . for bullying."

Bullying? But—but it was Jimmy who was the bully, not him! He had just been trying to put a stop to it!

"That's what I said—bullying. Yes, ma'am. You'd better come down here as soon as you can."

Sitting there with his mom on one side of him and his dad on the other, Derek stared down into his lap. He listened as Mr. Merckling explained what Derek had done to Jimmy. Derek realized that that was how everyone must have seen it, and he felt deeply embarrassed.

But if he was honest with himself, he was not ashamed. He had been sticking up for his little sister, whom he loved deeply. He had defended her against a bully who had made her feel lousy for weeks! But of course nobody knew that—not Mr. Merckling, not his mom, not his dad— not anybody else but him, Jimmy, and Sharlee.

"I . . . I just don't know what to say," said Derek's mom

after Mr. Merckling had finished his tale of woe. "I'm shocked! This is not like Derek at all."

"My apologies," said Mr. Jeter. "I thought I'd taught my son better behavior than this. I can promise you it won't happen again."

That made tears spring to Derek's eyes. He knew his parents' eyes were on him, but he couldn't look back at them. Not yet. Not until he'd had the chance to explain himself.

"Do you have anything to say for yourself, young man?" Mr. Merckling asked. "I hope you're ashamed of how you handled yourself."

Derek sighed and wiped his eyes. He sniffed and did not look up. "To tell you the truth, I feel like I did what needed to be done."

"Needed to be done?" Mr. Merckling repeated.

Derek looked up to see all three of them looking at him like he was from Mars.

"He was messing with my little sister," Derek explained. "I had to do something."

"What exactly do you mean, 'messing'?" his dad demanded, his tone somber and angry.

"He was taunting her, and telling other kids not to play with her, and he—he spit on her, and tripped her so she scraped her knee."

"I see," said Mr. Merckling. He thought for a moment,

then said, "Well. Derek, I think you know that the way you dealt with the situation is not acceptable."

"Yes, sir," Derek said, nodding. "I do know that. I just . . . I was just so *angry* that I couldn't see any other way to deal with it."

Mr. Merckling cleared his throat. "I'll tell you what. . . . If I can verify that your story is true and Jimmy has been picking on your sister, since this is the first time you've had any behavior issues of this nature . . . since no one was hurt, and since I see what caused you to misbehave so badly, I will let it go this time without a suspension from school."

Derek's heart skipped a beat. He couldn't believe he wasn't being suspended. What a relief!

"However, since this involved our school buses, I'm going to have to forbid from using the school bus for the next two weeks."

"What?" Derek was stunned. That meant his parents would have to drive him to school! Derek knew they both had busy schedules and didn't need to be burdened with the extra job of driving him to school.

"As for the rest, I'm going to leave that up to your parents. Mr. and Mrs. Jeter, I can see I'm putting Derek's consequence in good hands." He rose and shook their hands.

"Thank you, sir," said Mr. Jeter.

"You won't be sorry," said Derek's mom. "We'll take care of it."

No, Mr. Merckling wouldn't be sorry. It was *Derek* who was going to be sorry—that much, he was sure of.

In a way, he understood. Technically what he'd done to Jimmy was bullying, he could see that. But what else was he supposed to have done?

"I hope you're reflecting hard on what just happened," his mother said as they sat in the car on the way home. Sharlee was over at Aunt Dimp's, being babysat while the rest of the family dealt with this crisis.

"I'm really sorry, Mom and Dad," Derek said. "Sorry that you guys have to drive me to school now."

"Never mind that," his dad said sharply. "What about what you *did*?"

"I had to protect Sharlee, didn't I? That kid was making her life miserable! I'm being punished for bullying when it's Jimmy who was the bully!"

"You should have come to us first, Derek," his mom pointed out. "You should have known to do that."

"But—"

"But what?" his dad broke in. "There are no exceptions when it comes to doing the right thing."

"Sharlee made me promise not to!" he blurted out.

There was a moment of silence before his mom said, "Since when does a five-year-old force you to promise her anything? Especially something that's not good for her?"

Derek had no answer for that one. Nor did he have much to say when, after they got home, his dad brought out Derek's contract. "We're going to go over this again, to see just where and how you broke the rules."

Oh no! Up until that moment, with all that had been going on, he hadn't even thought of his contract.

Now the real impact of what he'd done began to sink in. The contract he'd made with his parents the year before was the glue that held his lifelong dream together! It was part of their solemn pact. They stood solidly behind his dreams, and he kept strictly to his agreements about his own conduct.

His dad pointed to three different rules: "Be a Role Model for Sharlee. Respect Others. Respect Yourself." He shot Derek a glance. "I'd say you've broken all three of those. What do you think, Dot?"

"I agree," said Mrs. Jeter. "By taking matters into your own hands, and being threatening, if not violent, you've set a bad example for Sharlee. You've shown no respect for school rules, or for the teachers whose job it is to enforce them."

"Let me remind you, Derek, that aggressive and intimidating behavior is never a good way to handle problems," said his dad. "It's what gets many young people into trouble so deep that they never get out of it."

"And another thing," his mom added. "If you ever have an issue, you're always to come to us first about it and get our guidance. No matter what other so-called promises you may make."

"Yes, Mom," Derek said humbly. He knew they were

right, as usual. He needed to think before he acted. "I'm sorry. It won't happen again."

"I'm sure it won't," said his dad. "Now. As punishment . . ."

Uh-oh, thought Derek. *Here it comes.*

"Because of this serious breach of your contract, you now lose the right to go to the Yankees-Tigers game in Detroit next month."

"NOOO!" Derek moaned. "No, please—not that!"

"You can't get any rewards for good behavior in the past," his mom said. "Not after this."

"And the *next* time anything like this happens," his dad said, "there will be no more baseball this season. Understood?"

"Yes, sir," Derek said, totally crushed.

He'd been looking forward to going to that game more than *anything*!

"We're also going to add one more item to your contract," said Mr. Jeter.

"Think of it as the First Amendment," his mom added.

"It's a short one, so you shouldn't have any trouble memorizing it," his dad went on. "It reads, 'Think Before You Act.'"

"Okay," Derek said, nodding. "I get it. Will do."

"And . . . ," his dad continued.

Uh-oh. There's more?

"Tomorrow morning you are to apologize to Jimmy face-to-face."

Derek felt like he'd been punched in the gut.

"You're going to walk into Mr. Merckling's office, with Sharlee, and you're going to show her the *right* way to handle things."

"But—"

"No buts," his mom said. "Now I'm going to go pick Sharlee up at Aunt Dimp's house. I'm going to tell her that Dad and I are glad she confided in you, but that she needs to be able to confide in us, too."

"That goes for you, too, Derek," said his dad. "You need to be able to trust us. You know you can always come to us about anything. You never need to feel embarrassed about it, and neither does Sharlee."

Chapter Thirteen

BREAKING THROUGH

The next morning Derek's parents drove him and Sharlee to school. As they got out, Derek saw Jeff standing at the bottom of the steps that led to the school's main entrance.

Jeff saw them too. "Hey, dude, what was up with that fight yesterday? You really scared the daylights out of that kid!" He laughed, clapping Derek on the back.

"It's not funny, man," Derek said seriously. He tilted his head toward Sharlee. "She doesn't need to hear that."

Jeff seemed to understand. "Got it," he said, winking.

"No, no. I mean . . ." Derek sighed. "I shouldn't have done it. It was stupid and just wrong."

"What, 'cause he's in first grade or something?" Jeff asked. "Yeah, I guess—"

Derek shook his head. "No, man. I mean it was wrong, period. I just wasn't thinking, and now I've got to deal with it." He put an arm around Sharlee's shoulder. "Come on, Sis. We've got places to go. See you later, man."

He led her down the hall toward the principal's office. Sharlee, who'd been silent until now, suddenly said, "I don't care what anybody thinks. I'm glad you did it. Thanks for sticking up for me, and for not telling Mom and Dad."

Derek stopped walking. He knelt down and took Sharlee by the shoulders, looking right into her eyes. "No, no, no," he said. "You've got it all wrong. I messed up, big-time. And now I'm paying for it. It was wrong not to tell Mom and Dad. None of this would ever have happened if we had. And it was wrong for me to pull that stuff with Jimmy—it's not going to help solve your problem."

"Yes, it will!" Sharlee insisted. "He'll be scared to mess with me now."

Derek shook his head again. "That's not the best way to get it to stop, Sharlee. I've been thinking about it. I *should* have thought about it *before* I went after him, but I didn't. I got mad and forgot to think until it was too late." The bell rang for the start of classes. "Speaking of late, come on. Let's get going."

He led her to the principal's office. Mr. Merckling had clearly been waiting for them. "Very good. You're here," he said. Pressing a button on his intercom, he said, "Please send Jimmy Vickers down here."

Two long, long minutes later Jimmy walked in. When he saw Derek, he nearly shrank right back out of the room. Obviously nobody had warned him Derek would be there.

Derek felt a pang of regret go through him. He could see how scared Jimmy was, just as scared as Sharlee must have been when Jimmy had been threatening her.

"I'm not going to hurt you," Derek assured him as Jimmy peeked around the edge of the door. "It's okay. Come on back in."

Mr. Merckling nodded approvingly, and Jimmy slowly came back in, keeping as far from Derek as he could in the small office.

"I wanted to say I'm sorry," Derek told him. "I mean, yeah, they told me I had to, but this is coming from me— for real. I really am sorry . . . okay?"

Jimmy stayed frozen for a moment, his terror of Derek only slowly going away. Then he nodded.

"I . . . I was just so mad—so upset when Sharlee told me what was going on with you and her that I—I kind of exploded and went off on you. I should have realized that talking to you would be better."

Everyone was silent, their eyes on Derek as he struggled to find the right words to say. "I . . . I love my little sister more than anything," he said, swallowing hard. "And I want everything to be good for her. I know not everyone can be best friends, but I'm her big brother, and I don't want anybody to hurt her, okay?"

Jimmy nodded, faster this time.

"So . . . I mean . . . you should just realize, Sharlee's an amazing kid. She's funny, and smart, and cheerful, and really, really good at sports. So you shouldn't make her miserable. In fact, you should want her on your team. I mean, it might help you win, right?"

Derek tried a smile, but it was hard, because he felt more like crying. He hated having to do this, especially in front of the principal, but he knew it was something he had to do. He owed it to Sharlee to show her the right way to handle the situation.

"I don't feel good about how it all went down," he said. "So I'm saying, I'm sorry, it won't happen again—and I hope you'll give what I said some thought. I mean, I was being a bully, but so were you. Maybe we can both do better. . . . Right?"

Jimmy bit his lip and gave a very quick, very little nod.

"You really should get to know Sharlee better," Derek said. "If you did, you wouldn't want to pick on her. You'd want to be her friend. I'm pretty sure of it." He sighed, looked up at the principal, and said, "I guess that's it. Okay?"

Mr. Merckling nodded appreciatively. "Okay. That was fine, Derek. Really, really fine." He turned to Jimmy. "All right, young man. Derek is offering you an apology. Do you accept it?"

Jimmy nodded quickly.

"Then shake hands, boys. And let this be the end of any kind of bullying from here on in." They shook hands, and that was the end of it.

Back out in the hall Derek walked Sharlee to her classroom before going to his own.

"Well?" he asked her. "What did you think?"

Sharlee made a face. "It was okay," she said. "But I think *Jimmy* should have had to apologize to *me*."

"Hmm," Derek said thoughtfully. "Well, you never know. Maybe he will."

"I don't think so," Sharlee said. "He's not nice, like you."

"You never know," Derek said. "People can change." He hugged her and sent her into her classroom. "See you after school," he said.

He closed the door behind her and let out a sigh. Thinking about what had happened over the past twenty-four hours, he felt lighter, freer than before. He hoped he was right about Jimmy changing his behavior. But he knew he couldn't control that.

He could only control his own.

If Derek had thought the incident was over with his apology to Jimmy, he had another thing coming. That day after school everyone on Jeter's Hill wanted to know where he'd been that morning, and why he'd been so late for class.

Derek tried to worm his way out of telling them, but

then Isaiah arrived and said he'd seen Derek going into the principal's office. Derek wound up having to tell them the whole story, leaving out a lot of the more painful details, of course.

"Parnell was letting me have it all day about how sports leads to bad behavior," Derek told them. "That was the worst part."

"Well," Jeff joked, "look at the bright side. At least now you have your own personal driver, just like Dave Hennum."

"Yeah, and I have to listen to bad jokes like that about it, just like Dave," Derek said with a crooked smile. "Why don't you guys lay off him—seriously?"

The smiles on their faces faded. "Yeah, I guess we've given him a pretty hard time," Jason admitted.

"And he's not a snob, either," Derek informed them. "Right, Vijay?"

Ever since the day at the batting cages, Derek had wanted to ask Vijay about why he was afraid to be friendly to Dave when other kids besides Derek were around. Now, seeing his moment, he had put Vijay on the spot.

"Um . . . no, actually," said Vijay, clearly embarrassed. "I can confirm he is normal, like the rest of us. Maybe richer, but not a snob."

"What are you, friends with him?" Jeff asked.

Vijay shrugged, feeling Derek's eyes on him. "Yes. We are friends," he admitted. "Hey, why not? He's cool."

"He never played baseball in his life before this year," Jason said. "Never. You've got to admit that's weird."

"No, it isn't," Vijay said. "Where he comes from they all play golf. Where I come from they all play cricket. So what? It's all sports."

"I don't know if I would call golf and cricket sports," Jeff said. "I mean, what kid plays them?"

"People in different places do different things," Vijay explained. "If you go traveling, you will see. It doesn't mean they're weird. Maybe they would think we're weird, right?"

That got everybody laughing, and the serious mood was broken. They went back to playing ball. But later, after the others had gone, Vijay said, "Derek, I want to say that I'm sorry I let you and Dave down before."

"Huh?"

"You know," Vijay said. "I was afraid the other kids would stay away from me if I made friends with Dave. But I shouldn't have been afraid. After all, you weren't afraid to be his friend. Or my friend, when I first came here. So thank you."

"For what?" Derek asked.

"For giving me the chance to say so," said Vijay. "Thank you, my friend."

Chapter Fourteen

STREAK ON THE LINE

From that day on, everything seemed to fall into place. Sharlee seemed like her old self again. Derek lived through the two-week ban on riding the school bus. His grades were good, and he didn't get into any further trouble.

As for Dave, he had become a regular member of the gang on Jeter's Hill. Once Vijay declared to everyone that he was friends with Dave, everyone else kind of fell in line.

It helped that most of them were on the same Little League team. It helped even more that the Red Sox hadn't lost a game in three weeks!

Dave's hitting had improved, and so had his understanding of the game. He now knew which base to throw to, when to cover the bag at third, and how to adjust to different game situations.

He wasn't the only one either. Vijay had become a decent hitter too, thanks to the tips Derek's dad had given him. And as for Derek, he'd made only one out at the plate in the past three weeks, and that one out had ended a 9 for 9 hitting streak.

As his mom the accountant pointed out to him, "By the way, old man, did you know that in spite of your tough start, you're now hitting above .300 for the season?"

It was no wonder, then, with all that hitting, that the Red Sox now had a four-game winning streak, bringing their record to 10–3!

With one game left in the regular season, they were now in third place, one game behind the Indians for second, and two games behind the first-place Yankees. The Yankees had won it all last year and were undefeated this year. They had already beaten both the Red Sox and the Indians, so they were a lock for first place.

The Mets, in fourth place, had already won their final game this morning, but they still trailed the Red Sox by half a game. And since the Sox had beaten the Mets this season, with a win in their game today, they would finish ahead of the Mets and make the playoffs!

Today their opponent was the Royals, a team with a

losing record. But those same Royals were the only team so far this year that had beaten the Indians, so they were dangerous for sure.

Derek was confident the Sox could handle them, though. The way the team was playing, winning had become infectious.

Things started well, with Jeff mowing down the first Royals hitter. But then he gave up a sharp single followed by a walk, to put runners on first and second.

As usual in these pressure situations, Derek wanted the ball hit to him. He felt best when he was in control of things. And sure enough, a hard grounder came sizzling his way.

Derek knew this was a chance for a double play. He dove to his right and speared the ball, then sprang to his feet to make the throw—only to find that the ball was still on the ground!

Blood rushed to his head as he reached down to grab it. There was still a chance to make the play at first base, at least. But he rushed his throw, and it was wide, getting by Murph and going into foul territory!

By the time Vijay retrieved the ball and threw it back in, two runs had scored, and the hitter was standing on third base. Derek looked up at the sky, shaking his head. How could he have messed that play up so badly?

Glancing over at the stands, he saw his mom, dad, and Sharlee all yelling encouragement. "Hang in there,

Derek!" he heard his mom say over the crowd noise.

He blew out a breath and settled back in at short. The game had just started, after all. There was plenty of time for the Sox to come back. Plenty of time for him to redeem himself.

That was the great thing about baseball, his dad had often told him. If you just hang around and stay ready, you always get another chance to do better.

The Royals were up 3–0 before the Red Sox came to bat in the first. They nearly got one back in the bottom of the inning on Derek's double, but Cubby was nailed sliding into home plate on the play, and the rally fizzled with no runs scored.

But as the game went on, the Red Sox started chipping away. They scored in the second when Dave homered with the bases empty. They added another run in the fifth when Derek drove Cubby in from first with another double. And finally, still behind 3–2 in the sixth with only one out left, Isaiah came lumbering home from second on a single by Vijay to tie the score and send the game into extra innings!

Across Westwood Fields, on one of the other diamonds, Derek saw the Indians erupt into cheers as they sealed their victory over the Tigers. That meant the Red Sox had to win this game to have any hope of a playoff spot. A loss or a tie, and they'd be eliminated.

The rule was, no inning could start after seven o'clock.

After two extra innings the score remained the same. The sun had gotten low in the sky, and it was hard to see from the infield staring in at the plate, because the sun was in the fielders' eyes.

The ninth inning began at precisely five minutes to seven. This was the last inning, Derek realized. Their last shot. They had to have a win, and they had only one inning to do it!

He was now back at shortstop, after having pitched the previous four innings. His arm was dead tired. Coach Kaufman had taken him out as pitcher only because Derek had reached his pitch limit.

Now the pitcher was Buster. Luckily, the bottom of the Royals' order was up, and Murph was able to get pop fly outs against the first two hitters. The third, however, smacked a double to left.

After that, Buster seemed to get rattled. He walked the next two hitters he faced. Then he threw a fat strike to the next batter, who looped it over Derek's head.

Derek turned and ran, trying to keep the ball in sight over his shoulder. He dove for it—and somehow he came up with the ball!

A huge cheer erupted from the rest of the team, and from their supporters in the stands. As he ran back to the bench, both arms thrust high above his head in triumph, Derek heard people screaming his name—and knew it was his family cheering the loudest.

Now it was the Red Sox's turn. One last chance for a victory. One last turn at bat. One last shot at staying in the playoff hunt.

Derek hoped and prayed he would come up to bat. But for that to happen, two players would have to reach base first. Vijay led off with a strikeout, and Miles popped to second base. But Cubby, up next, smacked a clean single past the shortstop, who lost it in the sun and ducked for cover. Then Jason walked.

And that brought Derek to the plate.

He let two pitches go by that he thought were outside, but the umpire called them both strikes, and Derek found himself in an 0–2 hole, with only one strike standing between the Red Sox and defeat. . . .

The next pitch came in high, but not high enough for Derek to risk being called out on strikes. He swung, trying to stay in balance, but he got under the ball and popped it up behind second base!

Derek groaned in frustration—but then he saw that the second baseman was having trouble finding the ball in the glare of the sun. To Derek's surprise and delight, the ball glanced off his glove and hit the turf—just as Cubby crossed the plate with the winning run!

After the celebration and the usual handshakes, Vijay threw his arms around Derek and hugged him. "Wow!" he shouted. "That was incredible! Unbelievable! We're in the playoffs, man!"

"I know," Derek said, unable to stop smiling. "I can't believe it! I thought for sure they had that ball."

"And just think," said Vijay. "Remember all those line drives you hit that turned into outs during those other games?"

"Boy, do I."

"And here you go, winning the game on a cheap, dinky fly ball that happened to find the perfect spot!"

"Hey," said Derek, still grinning like a fool. "That hit wasn't cheap. I hit it there on purpose!"

Chapter Fifteen

ON THE EDGE

"How did you do?"

Gary and Derek were at their lockers, which happened to be right next to each other.

"I got a ninety-three!" Derek said, holding out his math final for Gary to see. Derek was proud of his grade—he'd worked hard for it—but he wasn't sure it would be enough.

Gary smirked and slowly pulled the test booklet out of his binder. There it was. "Ninety-nine."

"Oh well," Derek said, managing a smile. "I'm not going to go cry about it. You win. *Again*. But I'll get you next time."

"Yeah right," said Gary, tucking the test back into his binder, probably saving it for future framing. "You always say that."

"Hey, I did it . . . once."

"Right. A total fluke. But what do you expect, Derek? When you waste a good mind on sports, that's what happens. I keep telling you—"

"Hey!" it was Dave who interrupted him.

Derek had seen him approach, but Gary hadn't been facing that way. Gary jumped at the harsh tone in Dave's voice, and at the hand Dave laid on his shoulder.

"I heard that," Dave told him. "And let me tell you, you're dead wrong."

"What do you know about it?" Gary said, snorting.

"If it weren't for sports, I wouldn't have made a single friend around here."

Gary's mouth hung open. He obviously had no idea what to say. Neither did Derek.

"And oh, by the way," Dave said, pulling a finals booklet out of his book bag, "I got a one hundred, okay?" He showed it to Gary, whose jaw hung even lower.

Derek couldn't keep the grin off his face. *Take that, Parnell!* he thought.

"I had no idea you were that smart," Derek told Dave after Gary had wandered off, shaking his head in disbelief.

"I'm *not* that smart," Dave said modestly. "Chase makes me put in long hours studying, so . . ."

"Yeah," said Derek. "I think your one hundred has more to do with hard work than whether or not you play sports, huh?"

"Guess so."

"Speaking of which, we've got a game to play today."

"Like I need reminding!" Dave said. "I'll be there, ready to go. This is the playoffs!"

"Right." They high-fived and went their separate ways, both knowing that in less than two hours they'd be battling for a spot in the championship game!

Derek could feel the goose bumps on his arms and all up and down his back. He knew that it was possible his team might lose today, but he didn't let himself think about that. He knew it was no use letting negative thoughts into your mind. No, you needed to stay positive at moments like these, when everything was on the line.

It was hard to stay positive, though, after the Indians' pitcher set the Red Sox down one, two, three for five innings in a row—only one inning short of a perfect game.

Luckily, he had reached his pitch limit by league rules and would have to be replaced in the sixth. That was the only thing keeping the Red Sox in the game—that, and some great pitching by Jeff, matching the Indians' pitcher zero for zero.

Buster took the mound for the top of the sixth, replacing Jeff, as he, too, had hit his limit. Buster looked scared up there, and that made Derek nervous.

"You got him, Murph!" he shouted encouragingly.

On the first pitch the hitter proved him wrong, lacing a

triple to deep left-center. Derek swallowed hard. It looked as if the Indians would surely score now, with a man on third and nobody out.

Derek made a trip to the mound and put an arm on Buster's shoulder. "Don't be scared, man," he said. "These guys should be scared of you."

"But that guy just—"

"He's their cleanup hitter," Derek told him. "Best they've got. Don't worry about these other guys. They've got nothing. Just throw it right over and trust the rest of us to make the plays behind you." He clapped Buster on the back and returned to shortstop.

Buster let out a big breath, and threw the next pitch right by the hitter. That seemed to give him more confidence, and he wound up striking the batter out. "There you go!" Derek said. "Just like that!"

On the next pitch the hitter smacked a line drive to Derek's right. Lunging and diving, Derek made the stab for the out, saving a run!

Then, seeing the runner at third trying to scramble back, Derek threw to Dave—who was alertly covering third base, just like Derek had taught him.

Double play! Inning over!

The Red Sox whooped and hollered, but Derek and Coach Kaufman both had to remind them that the game was not over. It was still 0–0, and Buster had already reached his weekly pitch limit.

With Derek and Jeff also over their weekly limit, someone else would have to pitch for the Red Sox if the game continued into extra innings—someone who'd never pitched for them, even in practice!

It was now or never, they all realized. This had to be their inning.

It didn't start well, with Buster striking out. And then Vijay got overexcited and hit an infield pop-up for the second out. Just as Derek was starting to feel they were headed to extra innings after all, Miles got a clean single—his first hit in the last four games!

"Attaboy!" Derek yelled as Miles thrust both fists high over his head. Derek could relate. He'd had a horrific slump himself, and now he knew how it felt to break out of one.

Cubby followed with a slap single to left that he turned into a double, while Miles wound up on third.

Jason was next. He swung through two pitches, but then the Indians' pitcher threw one wild and inside. It hit Jason on the backside, sending him to first base, loading the bases—and bringing Derek to the plate, with everything on the line!

All his life he'd lain in bed at night dreaming of moments like this. Now he imagined himself hitting the ball hard. Solid contact. That was all he wanted. . . .

The first pitch was on the inside corner, and Derek let it go by for a strike. That was okay with him. He hadn't seen this pitcher before, and he wasn't going to swing at a pitch unless he knew he could hit it. Not with fewer than two strikes.

"Strike two!" yelled the ump, to Derek's shock and dismay. The second pitch had been down below his knees. Only Dave could have hit it.

Part of him wanted to argue with the umpire, but Derek knew that would only ruin his concentration. He needed to stay cool . . . stay positive . . . and now that he had two strikes on him, he needed to protect the plate.

He fouled the next pitch off. It was outside, but not by much, and he couldn't have risked the ump calling it a strike. He fouled another one off, and then another—and then another!

He was just barely making contact each time, but he was fouling off good pitches—ones that might have been called strikes if he'd let them go by.

Sooner or later, he knew, the pitcher would make a mistake and throw one over the heart of the plate, where he could—

"OW!" The pitcher had made a mistake, all right, but instead of throwing a hittable pitch, he'd hit Derek square on the shinbone!

"Take your base!" the ump shouted, pointing to first. Derek hopped there on one leg, grabbing his sore shin, while the Red Sox and their fans erupted in cheers as Miles scored the winning run!

Derek crossed the first-base bag still yelling, "Ow, Ow, OW!" He had to laugh, even though his leg still hurt enough to make him cry.

Getting hit on the shin hurt, for sure, but it had gotten his team into the championship.

What a way to be a hero!

That night before dinner, Sharlee was all smiles. "You think *you* had a good day," she told Derek. "Wait till you hear what happened to me in school."

"What? What happened, Sharlee?" he asked. "It must be pretty good to top me getting hit on the shinbone with a fastball."

"It is!" she chirped. "Guess who invited me to his birthday party?"

"Umm . . . I don't know," Derek said, furrowing his brow and stroking his chin. "The prince of Persia?"

"No, silly," she said, giggling. "Jimmy Vickers!"

"What?" Derek couldn't believe his ears.

"Yes!" she confirmed. "And guess what kind of party it is."

"I don't know," he said, laughing. "Tell me."

"A kickball party—and he wants me to be on his team!"

"Wow, Sharlee! How about that?" He gave her a big hug, and she squeezed him tight.

"It's all thanks to you," she said.

"Sharlee, don't go there. I should never have—"

"No, I don't mean that part. I mean when you said he should give me another chance."

"Oh. Yeah, I guess I did say something like that," he said. "Well, good. That's great."

"Um . . ."

"Something else?" he asked.

"I was thinking of inviting him over here to watch that Yankees-Tigers game on TV. You know, the one you can't go to?"

Derek winced. "Don't remind me," he said. "What makes you want to invite him to watch that?"

She grinned, showing her dimples, and swayed from side to side. "Jimmy says he's a Yankees fan too!"

Chapter Sixteen

WINNER TAKES ALL

The end of the season had arrived. It had happened so suddenly that Derek hadn't seen it coming. His attention had been riveted on the Red Sox run for the playoffs, and now it was all coming down to one final game. Tomorrow it would end either in a blaze of glory or in the flames of defeat.

The end of school had taken him by surprise too. For two weeks they'd been taking tests, and then one day there weren't any more tests to take. His grades were all As and B-pluses, though he wound up lagging behind Gary yet again.

It bothered Derek, but not too much. He'd long ago decided that sports were anything but a waste of time. Gary wasn't going to change his mind, either.

The main reason Derek wanted to beat him so badly was to prove that playing sports didn't mean you were stupid. But Derek also knew that the competition helped them both get better grades. And now, for next year, Dave was in the mix too!

On that Friday, when everyone got out at one o'clock and hung around to say their good-byes till September, Derek suddenly realized that next week he'd be heading for New Jersey, to spend the summer with his grandparents at their home on Greenwood Lake, as he did every year.

He was happy about it, of course. He loved his grandparents, and his grandma always took him to see the Yankees at the big ballpark in the Bronx. Those outings to see the Bronx Bombers were Derek's favorite time of the whole year. Every time he watched them play in person, it made his dream seem more real—that someday he too might be out there, starring at shortstop.

Tomorrow, though, it would be his job to help the Red Sox beat a team called the Yankees.

"Hey, Derek!" Dave called, coming down the school's front steps. "Slap me five, man. School's out for summer!"

They high-fived, then gave each other the secret handshake that only kids on Jeter's Hill used.

"You ready for the big game tomorrow?" Derek asked him.

"As ready as I'll ever be," Dave said. "And oh, by the

way, I got us a tee time for Sunday afternoon at the municipal course—just us and Chase, but if your dad wants to come . . ."

"Oh, wow," Derek said. He'd forgotten completely that he'd promised Dave he would switch to golf the minute the baseball season was over. "I guess we're really playing then, huh?"

"Did you think I wasn't serious?"

"What about clubs, though? I don't have any. They're expensive too, right?"

"No worries," Dave said with a grin. "You're shorter than me. You can use my old set."

"Thanks for reminding me," said Derek. "I'm not exactly short, you know. Just next to you."

"I can't wait to get out there," said Dave. "I'm gonna play every day this summer. It's so fun! You'll see. Once you try it, you'll forget all about baseball."

"*That*," said Derek, smiling, "is *not* going to happen."

He suddenly realized he'd never told Dave about being in New Jersey for the summer. "By the way," he said, and laid it on him, as gently as he could.

"Oh," said Dave, the reality dawning on him.

"But I bet you could get some of the other guys to play golf," Derek said. "Vijay for sure. Maybe even Jeff, Jason . . ."

"I don't know," Dave said, still dealing with the news of Derek's coming departure for New Jersey.

"Hey, and I'll be back late August," Derek said. "We can play all fall, you know? At least till it gets too cold."

That prospect seemed to brighten Dave's mood. "Anyway, first things first. Right, Derek? Let's win us a baseball trophy!"

"Now you're talking!"

This was, without a doubt, the biggest game Derek had ever played in. Nothing else even came close. If the Red Sox won, they would be champions!

Derek had never been a champion before. Not once. In fact, this was his first chance at being one, and he was determined not to let it go to waste!

Coach Kaufman gathered the team together before the game. "I'm looking around," he said, "at a fantastic bunch of guys. You kids have done yourselves proud, whatever happens today. So hold your heads up, give it all you've got, and above all, have fun!"

The team let out a ferocious cheer. And they *were* a team now. At the beginning they'd been just a bunch of kids. Some had been friends before the season; some, like Dave, had been new and had struggled to fit in.

But somewhere along the way they'd started to play like a team—and about the same time, they'd started winning. Now here they were, playing for all the marbles.

The Yankees were the home team, thanks to their

first-place finish. So Derek's Red Sox batted first. "Let's jump on 'em!" Coach Kaufman told them.

Derek nodded. Coach Kaufman might not have been the best coach in terms of teaching the fine points of baseball, but he was good at getting the team motivated. He was a really nice guy, too. Derek decided that all in all, he'd been a good coach, if not a great one.

That great coach—the one he hadn't had yet—was his very own dad, Derek knew. There he was, standing up and clapping, urging Derek and the Sox on to victory.

Next to his dad stood Derek's mom, with Sharlee jumping up and down next to her. "Go, Derek!" He heard her high, piercing yell above the rest of the crowd.

Everyone was here to see this game. Derek saw players from other teams in the league, some of them wearing their jerseys one last time. Of course, there were plenty of Yankees fans too.

The Yankees, for their part, looked quiet and confident— and why not? They hadn't been beaten yet—not even once. Why should they have expected today to be any different?

Derek set his jaw and gripped the handle of his bat. He was hitting third in the lineup, but he was already set to go.

Cubby started things off right with a walk. He'd had so many this season that it seemed like he was always on base—and stealing. Sure enough, before Jason even swung at a pitch, Cubby was standing on second base.

Jason drove him in with a single, and the Sox had the lead, 1–0. Now it was Derek's turn. He stepped into the box, nodded once in the direction of his family, and settled in.

Somehow he didn't need to calm himself down this time. Something about this moment was like being in a dream. . . .

CRRACK! The ball sizzled down the right-field line, and Derek was off and running. He was halfway to third before he realized that Jason hadn't kept going and tried to score! Derek had to scramble back to second base, disappointed that he hadn't driven in that second run.

It wound up being a big deal too, because the next three hitters—Jeff, Isaiah, and Dave—all popped out to the infield, stranding both Jason and Derek, and forcing the Sox to settle for a one-run lead.

It quickly disappeared in the bottom of the inning, as Jeff walked two men and then gave up a double. Now it was the Yankees who were in the lead, 2–1.

Derek led off the third with his second hit of the day, a clean single to center. He stole second on the first pitch to Jeff, who let the strike go by so Derek could get into scoring position. But that strike led to another, and another, for the first out—and Derek was still at second.

Isaiah hit a tapper to second, and Derek took off for third. He made it safely, but now there were two outs—and Dave was coming to the plate.

"Get into one, big guy!" Derek yelled, clapping his hands.

Dave nodded back at him. He'd heard. But could he come through in the clutch?

The first two pitches came in high and over the plate. Dave swung through one and let the other go for a second strike.

Derek winced. "Keep it level, Dave! Remember—level swing!" He sure hoped Dave was listening. . . .

The ball came in low—in fact, it was in the dirt—and Dave couldn't help himself. He swung, with his old, long, loopy swing—and sent the ball far over the left fielder's head.

"YESSS! *Home run!*" Derek screamed, looping his arm in a circle as he trotted home in front of Dave, who seemed to be positively floating around the bases.

3–2, Red Sox!

But not for long. In the bottom of the third, the Yanks came roaring back, scoring three runs off Jeff, who wasn't having his best game. He continued to walk people, and they hit him hard whenever he threw one over the plate.

Derek made two great plays at shortstop to save at least a couple more runs, but by the end of the third inning, it was 5–3, Yanks.

The game stayed that way for a while. Then, in the top of the sixth, the Red Sox took the lead again. Derek, with his third hit in four at bats, singled home Cubby and Jason. Two outs later Dave hit a line drive double to left, and Derek raced across the plate for the team's sixth run!

Buster followed with a strikeout to end the inning, but now the mighty Yankees were up against the wall, facing imminent defeat. Derek couldn't help feeling that victory was within their grasp. Just three more outs!

Just three . . . more . . .

It was soon clear that the Yankees were not going to go down without a fight. Their first hitter fought off six straight fastballs from Buster before lacing a double to right. The guy after him grounded out, but the next hitter smacked a long double, scoring the tying run.

Derek groaned, along with everyone else on his team and all their fans in the stands. Suddenly the tide had turned once more. On the mound Buster slumped, his head down, looking like he'd already lost the game.

"Come on, man!" Derek told him, running over to give his friend some encouragement when he needed it most. "You've got this. These guys can't touch you. Just reach back and throw it right by them!"

Buster didn't look Derek in the eye, but he did nod his head. And sure enough, he blazed three fastballs past the next hitter for the second out.

One more out, and they'd go to extra innings. There would be no tie today, whatever happened. It was only two in the afternoon on this warm, sunny Saturday in the middle of June. Plenty of time for lots of extra innings.

Somebody was going to win this game, and Derek knew

that with one more out, their chances were back to fifty-fifty again.

But the next batter walked, as Buster seemed to lose both the plate and his confidence. A wild pitch sent both runners flying, and now it was second and third.

Coach Kaufman told Buster to intentionally walk the next hitter, to load the bases and have a force play at any base. That way no tag would be necessary—just touching the base would get the third out of the inning.

Buster walked the hitter, and the next man came up. Derek set himself, ready to grab even the fastest line drive. "Hit it here," he murmured. "Come on, right here." He pounded the pocket of his mitt, feeling sure that the ball would come his way. . . .

But it didn't. It went rocketing into center field, where Cubby lay out trying to make the diving catch—but couldn't. The Yankees runner came home from third base with the winning run.

The game and the *season* were over.

Derek sank to his knees. He could feel tears spring to his eyes. They'd been so close! Soooo close.

Looking up, he saw that Buster was sitting on the mound, staring at his shoes. Derek realized he must feel worse than anybody else.

Cubby, Miles, and Vijay were walking in from the out-field, watching the Yankees as they celebrated, mobbing one another along the first-base line.

Coach Kaufman gathered them all together. "All right, guys. I know you feel bad. I feel the same way."

Derek could see that it was true. Coach Kaufman really did care—the sight of his team so downcast had brought him to the brink of tears too. "But you played a great game. You showed everyone what you were made of. I'm proud of each and every one of you, and you should be proud too."

Maybe on another team, in a moment like this someone would have said something bad, like "This stinks," or "So-and-so messed up." But nobody on this team was going to blame someone else for the loss. They'd gotten this far as a team, and they'd gone down as a team.

When it was all over, and the two teams had finished shaking hands, it was time for the league commissioner to hand out the trophies to the champs.

This part was hard for Derek to watch. He felt such a letdown, after all his hopes and dreams of a championship had so quickly vanished.

Looking up, he was surprised to see his mom by his side. "Hey, old man," she said, giving him a kiss on the head. "Great game today. You guys played your hearts out."

Derek didn't answer. He just stared at the Yankees, holding their trophies high.

"Look, I know you feel bad right now," she said, squatting down by his side and taking his arm. "Just remember, it's a long road you're on. This is just one tiny stumble, and believe me, there'll be plenty more of them. If you want to get where you need to go, it's just part of the journey. Better learn to be okay with it."

"How?" Derek asked in a plaintive voice. "What am I supposed to do? Enjoy losing?"

"Of course not," his mom said. "But hey, think about your whole season. Your team made the playoffs. That's the first time ever you've made a playoff!"

Derek shrugged, and nodded. He had to admit, that much was true. It was progress, for sure.

"And you guys nearly won today. PS, you went three for four in your first playoff game. That gives you a .750 playoff batting average. Not too shabby."

Derek had to laugh, as sad as he was feeling. His mom, always with the facts and figures.

"You hit above .350 for the season, old man," she went on. "And you guys had fantastic team spirit. Some great wins this season. Great wins. And what did you make, one error at short all year?"

Derek nodded, smiling now for real. His mom had a way of always seeing the bright side—and making everyone around her see it too.

"Not for nothing, don't forget that last year you didn't even get to play short most of the time! *And* you got to pitch a bunch this year too. Not too shabby."

"Okay, okay," Derek told her, giving her a hug and a kiss. "I get the point."

"I'm not done yet," she said. "You had a heck of a year, and I just want you to get it. An A-minus average . . . a new friend . . . Plus, you learned a couple hard lessons, right? Like how to be a role model for your sister, for instance. And how to think before you act. Am I right?"

"You're right, Mom," Derek said. "As usual." He cracked a teasing smile, and she laughed and kissed him on the head again.

"If you want to achieve your big dreams someday, Derek, you can't let one loss get you down." She clapped him on the back. "Okay, old man, enough's enough. Go see your friends. Oh, by the way, I hear you're playing golf tomorrow, huh?"

Derek's smile vanished. "Oh. Right. I kind of forgot. . . . I don't really feel like it anymore, honestly," he said.

"Never mind," she said sternly. "You did tell your friend you'd go, didn't you?"

"Yeah, but now . . ."

"Now you don't feel like it? So, you're just going to do whatever you feel like, even if it hurts your new friend's feelings? "

Derek hadn't thought of that, but of course it would totally hurt Dave's feelings if Derek didn't go. "I guess you're right." Dave had supported him when he'd been in his batting slump, and Derek was going to return the favor by cheering on Dave's big drives and long putts.

"Listen, old man," his mom said, "get yourself out on

that golf course tomorrow and have fun. Hit a ball hard. Compete! You *like* competing, remember?"

Derek laughed. There was no doubt about it, he was as competitive as anyone else he knew—even in his own family.

"And besides, taking your frustrations out on a golf ball might make you feel better."

They walked over to where Dave was standing with Chase and Derek's dad, who was holding Sharlee by the hand.

"Great game, old man," his dad said, shaking his hand solemnly. "You're really getting somewhere. Lots of big improvements—especially up here." He pointed to his head. "Proud of you, boy."

"Thanks, Dad," Derek said. "And next year, remember— you're coaching. Right?"

"Me? Coaching?" Mr. Jeter frowned. "Did I say that?"

"YESSS!" Dave and Derek both shouted.

"He's my witness," Derek said, pointing to Dave.

"I'll tell you what," Derek's dad said. "I'll coach you boys next season . . ."

"Yesss!" Derek hissed.

"*If . . . IF . . .*"

"If what!"

"If Mr. Bradway will be my assistant coach."

"Me?" Chase looked like he'd been taken totally by sur- prise. "Well . . . Why . . ."

"Do it, Chase!" Dave urged. Turning to Derek and Mr. Jeter, he added, "Chase was a star baseball player in high school, you know!"

"Say yes!" Derek begged. He had to admit, people were full of surprises and hidden talents. At any rate, Chase sure was.

"Well . . . I suppose I will if you will, Mr. Jeter. But you'd better call me Chase. After all, everyone else does."

"Hmm. Well, in that case, you'd better call me Charles," said Derek's dad.

The two men shook hands on it, and Dave and Derek leapt into the air with excitement, and high-fived.

"What are you two so happy about?" Vijay said, coming up to them. When they told him, he was practically beside himself. "Wow! I sure hope I'm on the same team as you guys!" he said.

"Hey, Vijay, if I get a vote, you go where I go," said Derek. "And that goes for you, too," he told Dave.

"Like I said," said Mrs. Jeter. "It's the Three Musketeers."

Chapter Seventeen

FORE!

"I've got to say, I'm impressed with myself."

Dave laughed. "You've hit a few pretty good shots, my man," he said. "That drive had to be a hundred and forty yards." He lined up his drive and asked, "You having fun?"

"Man, am I ever!" Derek said. "It's kind of shocking, actually. On TV it looks like a total bore."

"See? What did I tell you?"

"Yeah, but I thought, to have fun at golf, you have to be insanely good, like you. You sure you're only ten years old?"

"I'm not *that* good," Dave said. "I've only won one tournament—last year back in Beverly Hills."

"Hey, that's one more championship than I've got," Derek pointed out.

"You're gonna get your share," Dave said, looking at Derek and nodding slowly. "I see how you are. You're like me. You work and work and work at it, and you never give up on your dream."

"That's it," Derek agreed. "I guess we've got a lot in common." He stepped back. "Your shot."

He really had surprised himself today. As they drove on the ninth and final hole, Derek had played more than a handful of really good shots for a kid his age. He'd even sunk a couple of difficult putts. Of course, there were plenty of shots he'd hit terribly—or missed altogether. But he'd done well enough to want to try again and do better.

Dave, for his part, had been amazing—drives of more than a hundred and fifty yards, long putts that had gone into the hole or just to the rim, even an amazing iron shot from a hundred yards away that landed just a foot from the hole.

"Chase must be a fantastic coach," Derek said.

"Yeah, he used to be on the pro tour, after he got out of the Special Forces."

"Wow," said Derek, impressed.

"Your dad's a pretty great coach too," Dave said.

"Next year we're going to have an outstanding team, with the two of them on board, huh?"

"I can't wait," Dave said.

"What? What? Did I just hear Jack Nicklaus say he can't wait for *baseball* season to start?"

"Oh, and Dave Winfield didn't just admit how much fun *golf* is?"

Derek watched as Dave sent another long shot right down the middle of the fairway. He knew right then that he would never be as good at it as Dave, but that was okay. Derek had discovered another sport he loved, one that he could enjoy for the rest of his life, even if he never won a championship at it.

Even more important, he now had *two* best friends instead of just one—Vijay and Dave. And he was sure those friendships would last a lifetime too.

RED SOX OPENING DAY ROSTER

Cubby Katz—CF

Jason Rossini—2B

Derek Jeter—SS

Jeff Jacobson—P

Isaiah Martin—C

Dave Hennum—3B

Buster Murphy—1B

Vijay Patel—RF

Miles Kaufman—LF

Reserves: Rocco Fanelli, Reggie Brown

Coach: Marty Kaufman

JETER'S LEADERS

is a leadership development program created to empower, recognize, and enhance the skills of high school students who:

- ◈ **PROMOTE HEALTHY LIFESTYLES AND ARE FREE OF ALCOHOL AND SUBSTANCE ABUSE**

- ◈ **ACHIEVE ACADEMICALLY**

- ◈ **ARE COMMITTED TO IMPROVING THEIR COMMUNITY THROUGH SOCIAL CHANGE ACTIVITIES**

- ◈ **SERVE AS ROLE MODELS TO YOUNGER STUDENTS AND DELIVER POSITIVE MESSAGES TO THEIR PEERS**

"Your role models should teach you, inspire you, criticize you, and give you structure. My parents did all of these things with their contracts. They tackled every subject. There was nothing we didn't discuss. I didn't love every aspect of it, but I was mature enough to understand that almost everything they talked about made sense." —DEREK JETER

DO YOU HAVE WHAT IT TAKES TO BECOME A
JETER'S LEADER?

- ○ I am drug and alcohol free.
- ○ I volunteer in my community.
- ○ I am good to the environment.
- ○ I am a role model for kids.
- ○ I do not use the word "can't."
- ○ I am a role model for my peers and younger kids.
- ○ I stand up for what's right.

- ○ I am respectful to others.
- ○ I encourage others to participate.
- ○ I am open-minded.
- ○ I set my goals high.
- ○ I do well in school.
- ○ I like to exercise and eat well to keep my body strong.
- ○ I am educated on current events.

CREATE A CONTRACT

What are your goals?

Sit down with your parents or an adult mentor to create your own contract to help you take the first step toward achieving your dreams.

For more information on JETER'S LEADERS, visit
TURN2FOUNDATION.ORG

Turn the page
for a sneak peek at
Change Up.

I can't believe it. My dream is finally coming true!

Derek Jeter sat in the back of his family's old station wagon, thinking those words, not saying them out loud, as he watched his dad get behind the wheel and fish out his car keys.

Instead Derek said, "Thanks for doing this, Dad. I know how busy you are, but I'm reeeeally happy you're coaching our team." *Finally,* he wanted to add, but stopped himself.

"I'm as excited as you are, Derek," Charles Jeter said, smiling as he glanced at his son in the rearview mirror. "It's the first time I've ever coached a team."

"Really?" Derek was shocked, although he probably shouldn't have been. Mr. Jeter had been a college player until he'd injured his knee, but since then had been working, studying for advanced degrees, and raising a family. Still, Mr. Jeter had been Derek's unofficial coach practically since Derek was in diapers. It seemed weird that his dad had never coached a baseball team until now.

"Wow! We get to be your first team," Derek said proudly.

"I just hope you'll be as happy about it when the season's over as you are right now. You might not be, if we wind up in last place."

Was he joking? Derek wondered. Probably. His dad always kept a straight face, so it was sometimes hard to tell what was a joke and what wasn't. But *would* Derek still be happy if their team wound up in last place?

That was not going to happen, he reassured himself. Never in a million years. His dad was the best coach in the world! Or at least the best Derek could ever imagine. Who else could have taught him so well, and cared so much, and believed in him so totally? His dad knew everything there was to know about baseball, Derek was sure of that.

Suddenly he remembered something. "Hey, Dad, don't forget to pick up Vijay at his house!"

Vijay had been Derek's best friend since the Patel family had arrived in Kalamazoo and moved into Mount Royal Townhouses, just a stone's throw from the Jeter family's townhouse in the same development. The Patels were from India, and they were the first Indian-American family Derek or any of the other local kids had known.

Derek had been Vijay's first friend in town, and they'd been best friends ever since. And now they were on the same team—for the third year in a row!

Derek's *other* best friend, Dave Hennum, was on the team too. In fact, the entire universe seemed to be aligning to produce the one thing Derek had never experienced in his baseball life—a championship team.

Vijay was already out in front of his house, waving both hands. His mitt was on his left hand, but that didn't stop Vijay. He was the king of excitement, as always.

"I can't believe it!" he said breathlessly as he plunked himself down in the seat beside Derek. "Slap me five. We're going all the way this time!"

Derek gave him five, but he wished Vijay wouldn't always make big predictions like that, at least not out loud. Derek thought it was bad luck to act like you'd already won something when you hadn't even stepped onto the field yet. In fact, neither he nor Vijay even knew who most of their teammates were!

But that was about to change. Every year at this time Derek practically held his breath as he waited to see who was on his team. But this year he was especially excited, so he could hardly blame Vijay for bursting at the seams.

In the back of the station wagon were two big duffel bags full of baseball equipment—everything the Indians would need, including balls, bats, helmets, and catcher's equipment. There were also maroon-and-gray Indians uniforms, socks, and hats in two big plastic garbage bags.

Vijay always saw the bright side of things. It was one of the main reasons Derek liked him so much.

"You boys ready to get to work?" Mr. Jeter asked them. "While it may be all fun for you, it's not all games with me and Mr. Bradway. We're going to put you through your paces. Got to be in shape if we're going to compete."

"You mean you are going to make us *exercise*?" Vijay asked. "Don't worry. We are already in shape from gym class!"

Mr. Jeter laughed. "We'll see. Coach Bradway and I were both in the army, remember? We may just put you kids through boot camp, so watch out."

They all laughed. Derek could tell that his dad was just as excited as the two boys. This was the day he would meet his first-ever team, the kids he would be responsible for all season long. It was a big job, and Derek could see that his dad, while joking around, was still taking his task very seriously.

They parked by their assigned field at Westwood Little League. The boys helped tote the equipment bags over to the home bench and lined up the bats and helmets along the fence.

"Why don't you two go toss it around for a few minutes? We're still early," said Mr. Jeter, taking out his notepad and pen. "Ah, good. Here comes Mr. Bradway."

The big Mercedes pulled up behind the Jeter station

wagon, and out scrambled Dave. Derek's mom had already dubbed the boys the Three Musketeers. Dave ran over to Derek and Vijay and got right into their game of catch.

Mr. Bradway—or "just Chase," as he instructed everyone to call him—was the Hennum family's driver, and Dave's caretaker while his parents were away on business, which was often. He got out and joined Mr. Jeter. Together they looked over their rules, schedules, and roster sheets. Practice wasn't scheduled to begin for another fifteen minutes.

Dave was as excited as everyone else. "We're riding a winner this season, guys. I can feel it."

"There is no doubt," Vijay agreed. "We are coming in first place for sure!"

"Hey, now. Let's not get overconfident," Derek warned. "We still have to play the games, remember?"

"Yeah, yeah, I know," Dave said. "But come on, Derek. Admit it. You feel it too."

It was true. Derek did have the strong feeling that they were going to be something special.

"I mean," Dave added, "it can't be for nothing that we all got on the same team again, *and* that your dad and Chase are coaching."

"It's too good to be true!" Vijay exulted.

That's just it, Derek couldn't help feeling. As psyched as he was, it did somehow feel *too* good to be true. He was only ten, but Derek already knew that life didn't usually hand out gobs of ice cream without at least a small help-ing of spinach on the side.

The thing that made him particularly nervous was that his dad had refused to show him the roster sheet when it had arrived in the mail the day before. "League rules," he'd said when Derek had begged to see who else was on the team. "You'll find out soon enough."

But his *dad* knew *now*, Derek thought. And that was driving him crazy.

"Hey, look. It's Harry and Josh!" Dave said, pointing. "Here they come."

"Do you think—" Vijay began hopefully. "Harry and Josh are ace players. If they are on the team, it will be fantastic!"

But they didn't stop at field number four. They waved, said "Hi," and kept on going, all the way over to field num-ber two.

Rats, thought Derek. *That would have been so cool. . . .*

Cubby Katz jogged by and waved hello, but he wasn't on the Indians either. The speediest kid in town wound up on field number three.

"Hey! Heads up!" Dave yelled. He was in the act of throwing the ball to Derek, who had stopped paying atten-tion in the middle of their game of catch.

Derek turned his attention back to Dave and Vijay so that he wouldn't get conked on the head. A few minutes later, when he turned to take another peek at the bench, there were a few kids gathered around his dad and Chase.

Derek recognized one of them. Jonathan Hogue was in his class at Saint Augustine's school, along with Dave and Vijay. Jonathan waved and smiled, and Derek was glad to see him. He was a nice kid, although Derek wasn't sure what kind of athlete he was. If he'd played in Little League before this, Derek had never run into him.

There were three other kids surrounding Chase, who was checking them in, then sending them over to Mr. Jeter for uniforms. "Hey!" Derek said. "If we want to get our favorite numbers, we'd better get over there!"

He sure hoped his dad had saved number 13 for him. It had been Charles Jeter's old number at college and had always been Derek's favorite for that reason.

"Did you save it for me?" he asked his dad.

"Wait your turn, Derek," Mr. Jeter said. "Go check in with Coach Bradway."

Derek was a little surprised that his dad was making him get in line like all the other kids who had just shown up. But he kind of understood. His dad liked to do things by the book, according to the rules—like not showing Derek the roster in advance.

"Hey, there's my main man!" Chase said, high-fiving Derek and checking him in. "You ready?"

"Always," Derek replied with a grin and a nod.

"Ha! That's the spirit. Okay, go get your new suit."

Derek got in line behind three other kids. He'd seen

them around in school, but he remembered only one from past seasons, a kid named Eddie Falk, who struck out a lot.

Looking around, Derek didn't see anybody from his mental wish list of teammates. One or two looked like they might be good athletes. But still Derek felt vaguely disappointed, and a little worried that the "sure thing" Vijay and Dave were imagining was starting to look a little shaky.

"There you go, Derek," said his dad, handing him uniform number 7.

"But—" Derek started.

"I know, I know," said his dad. "Thirteen is an extra large. Are you sure you still want it?"

Derek knew he was a size medium, if not small. He shook his head, disappointed again.

"Hey, number seven is Mickey Mantle's number!" Mr. Jeter pointed out. "The Mick! One of the all-time great Yankees."

That was true, Derek had to admit. There were a lot worse numbers.

"Besides, it's lucky. Lucky seven! Tell you what, Son. Whether you make your own luck, or you *need* a little luck, seven is your number." He gave Derek a smile and a wink, and Derek couldn't help smiling back as he took his uniform and hat.

"Okay, Indians!" Mr. Jeter said loudly, clapping his hands. "Let's gather round, shall we?" He introduced himself and Chase and said they were co-coaches. "Just call us both 'Coach,'" he instructed the team. "One of us will be sure to answer. Now let me have Coach Bradway read the roll call. Coach?"

"Derek Jeter?"

"Here."

"Dave Hennum?"

"Here."

"Vijay—"

"Right here!"

"Patel. . . . Jonathan Hogue. . . ."

He went on reading names. When all were accounted for, Chase said, "There are still three more names. Anybody know where Miles Kaufman is?"

Derek knew Miles. He'd been on last year's team and had improved as the season had gone on, but he was no all-star. Nice kid, though.

"Jonah Winters?"

"Here!" a kid yelled, running up to join the rest of them. He was carrying a baseball mitt like he'd never held one before.

"Gary Parnell?"

There was an audible gasp from at least three other kids besides Derek. But as for Derek himself, all he heard was the sound of a loud, terrible gong in his head. *The Gong of Doom.*

GARY PARNELL? Derek's biggest nemesis in school? The kid who beat him on nearly every test in every subject, and always, always rubbed it in? The kid who absolutely, positively hated sports, calling them a waste of a good brain and valuable time?

That Gary Parnell?

No. It couldn't be. There had to be another, some kid Derek had never met but who wasn't—

"Right here!"

That voice. It could only be . . .

"Are you Gary Parnell?" Chase asked.

"That's me. Unfortunately."

Derek turned around slowly . . . and there was his worst nightmare, being handed an Indians uniform and hat.

"Derek Jeter! As I live and breathe," said Gary. "Fancy meeting you here."

Derek stared. Gary looked as miserable as Derek felt.

"Why?" Derek whispered. "Why are you here? What are you, of all people, doing on a baseball field? I thought you hated baseball even more than you hate all other sports!"

"I do!" Gary confirmed. "I did, I do, and I always will. I'm just here to make your life intolerable."

"You're totally succeeding," Derek whispered, frowning.

"Seriously," Gary said with a sigh, "my mom is making me do it."

"Huh?"

"She's punishing me."

"For what? For getting only a ninety-nine on your last test?"

Gary smirked. "Feeble, Jeter. No. She insists I'm out of

shape and that I need to be more active. *Yecch*. All this 'active and healthy' stuff makes me want to puke." He stared at the uniform in his hands. "And they don't really expect me to dress up in *this*, do they? There is no way. Sor-ry."

This was a disaster of the highest proportions. Derek could feel the panic rising in his throat. He needed to scream—but of course that wasn't going to happen. He was just going to have to somehow overcome this . . . this catastrophe.

"Your mother is right," Derek managed to say. "You do need to get in shape. I mean, your brain might be in shape, but—"

"Yeah, yeah." Gary dismissed him. "I'll show her—and the rest of you too, while I'm at it. I'm going to use this unfortunate period of forced torture to prove once and for all that sports are a complete waste of time and belong in the dustbin of history."

Derek wanted to scream. He wanted to take an eraser and wipe this day clean so that he could start it all over and make it turn out differently.

But he couldn't do any of that. There was his dad, right over there. There was Chase. There were his friends. There were all these other kids who were going to be his teammates.

Derek knew he would have to accept this unacceptable, horrible mistake. But how in the world were he and the Indians supposed to even *contend* for a championship with *Gary Parnell* on the team?